The Jerry McNeal Series

Mystic Angel

(A Paranormal Snapshot)

By Sherry A. Burton

Also by Sherry A. Burton

The Orphan Train Saga
Discovery (book one)
Shameless (book two)
Treachery (book three)
Guardian (book four)
Loyal (book five)

Orphan Train Extras
Ezra's Story

Jerry McNeal Series
Always Faithful (book one)
Ghostly Guidance (book two)
Rambling Spirit (book three)
Chosen Path (book four)
Port Hope (book five)
Cold Case (book six)
Wicked Winds (book seven)
Mystic Angel (book eight)
Uncanny Coincidence (book nine)
Spirit of Deadwood

Romance Books*

Tears of Betrayal

Love in the Bluegrass

Somewhere In My Dreams

The King of My Heart

Seems Like Yesterday

"Whispers of the Past," a short story.

Psychological Thriller

Surviving the Storm

*A note from the author: With the exception of *Seems Like Yesterday* (which has been revised to be a clean read), my romance books have SEX. A couple of them have sex more than a few times. We are not talking close the door and turn off the lights sex. We are talking glow-in-the-dark condoms (*King of My Heart*). *Surviving the Storm* is a lot darker than my other titles and may not be for all readers. While I no longer write books where the lovemaking scenes are so detailed, I am not removing them from these early books, as the readers seem to enjoy them.

The Jerry McNeal Series

Mystic Angel

By Sherry A. Burton

The Jerry McNeal Series: Mystic Angel

By Sherry A. Burton
Published by Dorry Press
Edited and Formatted by BZHercules.com
Cover by Laura J. Prevost
@laurajprevostphotography
Proofread by Latisha Rich

For more information on the author and her works, please see www.SherryABurton.com

I will forever be grateful to my mom, who insisted the dog stay in the series.

To my hubby, thanks for helping me stay in the writing chair.

To my editor, Beth, for allowing me to keep my voice.

To Laura, for EVERYTHING you do to keep me current in both my covers and graphics.

To my beta readers for giving the books an early read.

To my proofreader, Latisha Rich, for the extra set of eyes.

To my fans, for the continued support.

Lastly, to my "writing voices," thank you for all the incredible ideas!

Table of Contents

Chapter One

If Jerry had learned anything in the time since he'd resigned from the State Police Post and set out on his own, it was to listen to his feeling. That was why he didn't hesitate to alter his course when his "feeling" urged him to venture into the town of Westerly, Rhode Island.

After having followed his instincts in and around the streets of the town, he now found himself staring at a red brick building in the heart of the city. The sign overhead showed the building to be home to a pizza restaurant. Gunter sniffed the air and licked his lips. That his ghostly partner was not currently dressed in his police vest was promising.

Jerry placed his hand on the door handle. "I guess we should go inside and see what's what."

Gunter led the way, stopping in front of a sign that read *Wait to be seated.* For a moment, Jerry thought the dog could read, then realized Gunter had merely keyed on a waitress clearing a table on the other side of the room. Though her back was to him, the energy surrounding the woman was one of troubled uncertainty. *Okay, McNeal, you're here.*

Now what?

The place was packed – all tables full except for the table the woman was cleaning. The waitress turned around and saw him standing there. A frown tugged at her lips. Jerry wondered if her disappointment was due to having another customer to tend to or the fact that he would be taking up a table that could have easily sat six.

She blew the hair from her eyes and managed a half smile. “Have a seat. I’ll be with you as soon as I can.”

Between him and the table in question were three tables pulled together. Each of the fourteen chairs was occupied, and from the empty plates and beverage bottles in front of them, it looked as if the group had been there a while.

Jerry started toward the empty table with Gunter at his side. A man at the combined table leaned toward him as he neared. “Word of warning, pal, the service sucks, and the waitress is a...”

Before he could finish, the woman sitting next to him elbowed him in the ribs. “Knock it off, Dan. The waitress is doing the best she can, and you are not helping any.” She shrugged and motioned to the beer bottles on the table in front of the man.

Instead of being deterred by the man’s warning, Jerry was even more convinced he was in the right place.

The man laughed and shook his head as Jerry

continued to his table. "No skin off my back, man. Don't say I didn't warn you."

As Jerry approached the table, he subtly pulled out the chairs, then sat with his back to the wall. Gunter made his way under the table and turned so that he was facing the room. *Good dog, forever watching my back.*

The waitress came out from the back, took the long way around the combined table, and made her way to where Jerry sat. Her dark hair was pulled back, and she'd fixed her wayward strands. With the exception of a touch of lipstick, her pale face was devoid of makeup, a good thing as her red-rimmed eyes made it clear she'd been crying. She offered him a menu. "I'm Susie. What can I get you to drink?"

Jerry waved off the menu. "I'll have a bottle of Bud and a pepperoni pizza."

She smiled. This time, it was genuine. "What size?"

"Large."

Another smile. "You've got it."

"Yo, waitress. Bring me another brewski."

Susie passed the table without acknowledging the man, placed the ticket in the window, walked to the cooler, and pulled out two bottles of beer. On her way back, she put a bottle in front of the man and continued on without comment. She approached Jerry, twisted off the cap, and placed the bottle on the table. "You want a glass?"

Jerry took a sip. "Nope."

"Hey, waitress. You're not being very nice. I'm going to remember that when I leave my tip."

Susie closed her eyes as if to steady herself.

Gunter shifted under the table. Jerry moved his leg to touch the dog in an attempt to settle him. "Do you know the guy?"

Susie shook her head. "I've never seen any of them before."

The pull he'd felt that led him there had now turned into a tingle that crawled across the back of his neck. Jerry looked over her shoulder. "Tourist?"

"Maybe. I just know they're not regulars. Your pizza shouldn't be much longer." She turned to leave and stopped by the table, collecting an armful of beer bottles. As she went to step away, Dan reached out and pinched her on her left butt cheek. Jerry was halfway out of his chair when Susie drew back her elbow, nailing the guy smack in the nose. The restaurant exploded in applause as the guy grabbed his face. When he brought his hands down, they were covered with blood, eliciting another round of cheers.

Jerry returned to his seat and smiled at Gunter, who still lay crouched beneath the table.

The reaction from those sitting at the table with the man were mixed. Half seemed incensed, and the other half seemed to feel the guy had it coming.

Jerry studied the girl sitting next to Dan, trying to gauge her reaction – there wasn't any. No gloating. No feigning concern. Nothing. The lack of reaction worried him nearly as much as the deep scowl on Dan's face.

Susie returned with a handful of napkins and the bill. Her face was now red, and her eyes brimmed with fresh tears as she placed the napkins on the table and mumbled her apology.

She didn't wait for a response as she went from table to table, apologizing to the other guests. Another ten minutes passed before she reached his table with a bubbling hot pizza. She sat the metal serving tray on the table in front of him. "I'm sorry."

"You have nothing to apologize for. The man was out of line." Jerry said loud enough to be heard.

Susie blinked back tears and kept her voice low. "Maybe not. But I'm not sure the owner will agree. They have a nice place here and want to keep their good reputation. It's not my fault service is slow. The other waitress went home sick a couple of hours ago."

Jerry looked toward the kitchen. "They couldn't call anyone in?"

"They did. But the girl has a kid and can't get here for another hour." Susie shrugged. "I thought I could handle it. It would have been fine if the guy hadn't drunk so much."

"I'd be glad to say a good word for you and tell

them what I saw."

Susie's lips quivered. "Thank you. I only have a week left before I head back to college."

An image of Rosie Freeman came to mind. Jerry rolled his neck.

"I was excited when that group first showed up as it had the potential for a nice tip. Now, I'm sure they will get out of here without paying their own tab. Sorry. I didn't mean to complain." She gave a weak smile and left, giving Dan a wide berth as she went to clear the table of a couple who was now at the counter paying their tab.

Jerry wasn't as worried about Susie's job as much as he was about her well-being. Dan had grown eerily quiet. Sitting sideways in his chair, his head pivoted, following the young woman's every move.

Jerry leaned back in his seat and started in on his pizza, which was exceptionally good. As he ate, the people at the triple table began to leave – except Dan and the woman sitting next to him. Though she didn't speak, the woman made no move to leave. *She's scared of him*. As soon as the thought came to him, Gunter growled. Jerry knew the dog to be agreeing with him.

Jerry studied the woman for any physical signs of abuse. There weren't any bruises on her face. The sweater she wore kept him from seeing her arms. *The sweater*. Jerry hadn't thought anything of it before. It was cool in the building, and she wasn't the only one with her arms covered. Several ladies seated around the room wore sweaters or had wraps draped over them. It was summer, and the air was often cool inside.

Still, something whittled at his senses. And that something told him if he let Dan walk out of here, someone was going to get hurt. Either he would stalk Susie to get his revenge or take his anger out on the woman sitting next to him who was doing her best not to draw attention to herself.

Jerry ran a hand over his head. *You need a plan, McNeal. Preferably one that won't get you arrested.* He finished his slice of pizza, wiped his hand on a napkin, and took out his phone. He studied the device, debating his next move. His first instinct was to call Seltzer, his go-to guy whenever he had a problem, and then decided against it. *Man up, McNeal, you need to stop creating trouble for the man.* He could call 911, but so far, the guy's only crime was not being able to control his liquor intake. Even that was debatable as the guy now appeared in total control. While he'd pinched her on the backside, Susie had done a fine job of handling that on her own. Only Jerry knew better. Picking up his cell, he hit redial, calling Fred's number. The man answered. Jerry lowered his voice. "You have anyone in Westerly?"

"Rhode Island?"

"Yep."

"What do you have?"

"I'd like to say it's nothing but my…" Jerry started to say "spidey senses" but reconsidered. "Something don't feel right."

"You sick?"

Jerry had to give it to the guy. His voice sounded genuinely concerned. "No, this is cop stuff."

"Something with my niece?"

"No. I haven't made it to Mystic yet."

"I didn't know you knew anyone in Rhode Island."

"I don't. Or didn't until a few moments ago. Listen, I don't have time for twenty questions. I have a situation brewing. Can you help or not?"

"Give me your location. I'll send someone."

Jerry rattled off the address and ended the call. He raised his hand to get Susie's attention and watched Dan as she approached. The guy swiveled in his chair and now sat facing them, watching their every move. Jerry kept his voice low. "Stay away from that table. No, don't look. You know which one I'm talking about."

"I've got to clean it."

"Not yet, you don't. Don't even go near it. I want you to wait for them to leave." Jerry didn't want to scare her but couldn't see any other choice. "I've got a bad feeling about him. He hasn't stopped watching you since you clocked him."

She looked Jerry in the eye. “These feelings; they ever come true?”

All the time. Jerry nodded. “Enough to tell you to stay clear of the guy.”

She rubbed at her arms. “My shift’s over in an hour. What if he doesn’t leave?”

“If he’s still here when it’s time for you to go, I’ll follow you home.”

Her right eyebrow lifted. “This better not be some sick new pickup line.”

Jerry smiled and shook his head. “I assure you I am not trying to pick you up.”

She sighed. “Too bad. I might have just let you.”

“Waitress, quit flirting and bring me another beer!”

Susie stiffened. “What do I do?”

“Ignore him. He gets out of that chair, and I’ll take him down myself.”

Her eyes flew open. “Are you a cop?”

Say no, McNeal. It’s not your fight. Then why am I here? Jerry rolled his neck. “Something like that.”

Susie’s shoulders relaxed. “Then why didn’t you say so? Geez, I feel better already. Wait, you’re not going to arrest me for smashing the guy’s nose, are you?”

Jerry shook his head. “I don’t arrest people. Besides, you weren’t even looking in his direction when it happened.”

Susie bit her lip and rushed off to seat a couple that had just entered. As she led them away, the door to the building opened, and a man stepped inside. Though he wore plain clothes, Jerry pegged the man as a cop the moment he entered. The way he paused just inside the door and scanned the room. The way his shirt bulged at his hip – giving just the hint of the gun hiding underneath. And the way the man's gaze took in every table before focusing on Jerry sitting alone at his.

Jerry lifted a finger, and the man started in his direction. Just before he reached Jerry, Dan pushed his chair back, screaming obscenities with drunken slurs. The cop pivoted and tapped Dan on the shoulder. Dan came around with a right hook, but the cop was ready for him, grabbing Dan's arm and twisting him around, slipping cuffs on his wrists before Dan knew what had happened.

The cop looked over at Jerry. "You McNeal?"

Jerry nodded.

"I'm supposed to give you a message."

"I'm listening."

"I was told to tell you that if you took the job offer, you could call for your own backup." The cop pulled Dan to his feet and looked at Jerry. "Anything else I can help with?"

Jerry shook his head. "That'll do it."

The cop grabbed Dan's arm, shuffling him toward the door. The woman who'd been sitting next to him grabbed her purse and hurried after them. Jerry wanted nothing more than to run after her and tell her she was making a mistake, but he remained seated. She was not who he was here for. Nor was she ready to heed his advice.

Chapter Two

Jerry sat in his Durango watching the front door to the building when the dash alerted him to a call. Recognizing Fred's number, Jerry accepted the call. "Yes."

"Did you get my message?"

"Yep."

"Ready to accept?"

"Nope."

Fred's sigh was audible. "You know, it would be a waste to let all that talent go unappreciated."

"I'm sure there are some that appreciate what I do. Susie, for instance. Did you get any word on the guy I called about?"

"Yes, it was a good call. The guy has had multiple assault charges. One for nearly killing a man."

"And yet he's still walking the streets."

"My guys are onto him now. We'll see he gets what he deserves."

"Is it going to take him almost killing someone to put him away?"

"Hopefully, we can intervene before it comes to

that."

The more Fred spoke, the more his neck crawled. "Where's the guy now?"

"They'll hold him as long as possible, but he'll probably be out on bail soon. Maybe you should have let the guy rough her up a little. Then we could have nailed him."

"I need you to put someone on his girlfriend."

"You're barking orders like you're one of us. I'd like to know you've officially taken the job before I take orders from a random Joe on the street."

Jerry ignored the comment. "I'm going to get the waitress out of town today. Dan is a loose cannon. If he can't get what he's after, he's going to find another punching bag. My gut tells me it will be the girlfriend."

"You'd set her up like that?"

The comment stung. It was an impossible situation. Jerry closed his eyes briefly before continuing. "The girlfriend isn't ready to leave."

"You think she will be if he smacks her around?"

"Doubtful. My guess is Dan's already crossed that line."

"So your solution is to use her as bait to put the guy away? Wouldn't it be easier to leave the waitress in play and give the guy what he really wants?"

An image of Susie lying at an odd angle flashed before his eyes. Jerry shook his head to rid himself of the image. "Nope. It wouldn't end well for her. The girlfriend has made her choice. We'll leave this to her."

"I didn't peg you to be so brutal, McNeal."

Doc's voice floated through his mind. *You can't save them all, McNeal.* Jerry interlaced his fingers and placed them behind his head. As he pulled on the back of his neck, he brought his elbows toward his face, in essence giving himself a hug.

"You still with me, McNeal?"

Jerry unclasped his fingers and placed his hands on the wheel. "I'm here."

"I was just kidding with that comment. It's a good plan."

"No, it's not, but it's the only one I can think of at the moment. Just make sure you have someone watching the girlfriend when they let the guy out. My gut tells me you won't have to wait long."

Gunter yipped. Jerry saw Susie heading across the parking lot. "I've got to go. The waitress is leaving, and I want to catch her before she gets in her car."

"Give me a call if you need anything."

Jerry ended the call and stepped out of the Durango just as Susie headed up the hill.

She jumped, then recognition set in, and she smiled. "You scared me. I guess I'm still a little wigged out by the guy."

"Are you parked nearby? I'll walk you to your

car."

She shook her head. "I don't have a car. I only live up the hill. It's not that far."

"Do you mind if I see you home safe?" Jerry smiled a disarming smile. It was important to gain the girl's trust, though he didn't yet know why. "No strings. I'm a cop, remember? Just doing my job."

Gunter moved past her close enough to brush against the woman's legs. Susie whipped her head around. She turned back to Jerry and nodded her agreement. Jerry was both pleased and troubled when she didn't ask for proof of his police ties.

Good boy, Gunter. The dog wagged his tail in response to Jerry's silent praise and lowered his nose to the ground as they started up the hill.

They'd taken several steps when Susie stopped. "I just realized you never told me your name. I know you're a cop, but you didn't tell me your name."

"And yet you agreed to let me walk you home."

"If you can't trust a cop, then who? Besides, I don't really feel like walking alone tonight."

"What if I had lied about being a cop? People do it all the time."

"I get that. But you look like a cop. Besides, that other cop knew you. I'm glad you called him."

"Why's that?"

"Because if you didn't, you wouldn't be here to walk me home."

"Where's school?"

"Massachusetts."

"You said you don't have a car. How did you get here?"

"I rode the train. The station's right down the street. Wait, you should know that if you live here."

Jerry laughed. "You're too trusting. I never said I did."

"But you knew the other cop."

"Actually, I know someone who knows him." *At least I think he does.*

"I should have asked for ID."

"Do you want to see my badge?" *Please say no.*

Susie shook her head. "No, I guess not. I doubt you would have called the cops if you were planning on doing something bad."

Jerry tried to relax, but his radar was pinging something fierce, the skin on the back of his neck crawling the whole way up the hill. So much so that he kept looking around to make sure they weren't being followed. He knew he was acting like a creep and kept waiting for her to call him on it, something she never did. They reached the top, and Susie turned left onto State Street. Gunter crossed the road in front of them, moved to the sidewalk, and picked up his pace. Jerry wondered what had caught the dog's attention as he continued to move forward, sniffing the stacked rock wall that lined the perimeter of the tree-filled park. It was a nice piece of property, dipping between the two streets.

Jerry tried to see beyond the trees. "That's a decent-size property."

"Wilcox Park is fourteen acres."

"I saw it when we were walking up Broad Street. Wouldn't it be closer for you to cut through?"

Susie followed his gaze and rubbed her arms. "It would, but I don't like doing that."

"You have a problem with shortcuts?"

"No." It was a simple answer, but all she seemed prepared to give. "I'll be glad to get back to college."

"You like school that much?"

"Yeah, I love it. But that's not the reason."

Gunter keyed on something in the rocks. His hackles went up as he pawed at an area near a large tree. Jerry stopped and looked at the dog.

"You really are psychic, aren't you?"

Jerry turned his attention back to Susie and saw her trembling. He frowned. "Are you alright?"

"Yes. It's just that spot really creeps me out."

The tingle increased. "Why is that?"

She bit at her bottom lip and began walking. "The way you were looking, I figured you already knew."

"I know something happened there but don't have the details." The fact that Gunter had keyed on the spot and was now looking in their direction told him Susie was involved.

"I was walking home one night, and a guy tried to grab me. He would have gotten away with it if I didn't have this." She opened her hand to show a palm-size container of pepper spray. "I zapped him with it and ran to the house across the street. By the time the police showed up, he was gone. It didn't surprise me as I saw him get into a van."

What started out as a tingle was now a full-blown crawl. *Easy, McNeal, don't get ahead of yourself. She's not a redhead.* Even though Susie didn't fit the profile, he knew. "What kind of van?"

"A big white one. You know, the kind they use for deliveries."

"Did you get a look at the guy?"

Susie stopped in front of a large white house with black shutters. "Yes and no. I gave his description to the police. This is where I live." She sighed. "At least for the next week."

"Susie, what did he look like?"

She shrugged her annoyance. "Yep. You're a cop, alright. It ain't going to help, though. The other cops told me so. Said I didn't give them enough to go on."

Jerry placed a hand on both her shoulders and looked her directly in the eye. "I don't care what they said. Tell me."

"Six feet with brown hair and eyes. He had a bald spot at the top of his head."

She was right. It wasn't enough for most crimes. But it matched the description they already had, which helped to confirm his own suspicions. The only thing that didn't add up – Susie didn't fit the killer's MO. While her complexion would have easily passed for a redhead's, Susie had dark brown hair. Jerry let go of her shoulders. *Better get a grip, McNeal. You're letting your imagination run away from you.* Jerry looked at the three-story house looming in front of them. He'd been so intent on connecting her near abduction to the Hash Mark Killer that he hadn't even noticed the stately home. "This is your house?"

She laughed. "Like I could afford a house like this. No, I rent one of the upstairs rooms. The stairs to the third-floor entrance are in the back and open to anyone who wants to climb them. That's why I didn't run here the night the guy tried to nab me. I didn't want him to know where I lived."

"Smart lady." Jerry jammed his fingernails into his palms. He wasn't wrong. He knew it as sure as he knew how to breathe. "Are you sure you don't remember anything else about that night?"

Her hand went to her throat. For a moment, Jerry thought she was going to tell him the man tried to choke her. "I lost my necklace in the struggle. It was a locket with a tiny picture of me and my mom."

"Did you tell the police?"

She nodded. "One of my friends said the guy who tried to nab me has it. I hope not. It kind of creeps me out to think he has a picture of me and Mom."

Me too. "Did the police look for it?"

"They looked around, but they weren't there very long."

Jerry looked down the street at Gunter, who was combing the area with his nose to the ground. "What about you? Did you ever look?"

Her eyes grew wide, and she shook her head. "I can't even bring myself to walk on that side of the road."

Gunter had found whatever it was he was looking for and was now digging at the dirt between the sidewalk and the rock fence. *He found it.* "Care if I have a look?"

She laughed. "It's been months. Even if it's still there, it's probably buried."

"Probably, but I'm psychic, remember? If it is there, I'll find it." The claim sounded like a farce even to him. But even as farfetched as it was, it was a far cry from telling her his ghost dog partner was digging it up this very minute.

"I've seen television shows where people do that. Would it help if you had something of mine to hold while you look?"

Jerry smiled. "Sure."

Susie opened her purse and pulled out her wallet. Opening it, she dug out a gold wedding band. "It was my mom's. I used to wear it on the chain with the locket. I had a bad feeling that day, and I took it off and put it on my finger. I guess it's a good thing I did, or it would have been lost along with the necklace. Do you think it will help?"

"It seemed to help keep you safe. I think it will do just fine." Jerry took the ring and placed it on his pinky with the intention of pretending to use it as a psychic divining rod. It could have worked if in fact he needed one. The truth of the matter was Gunter now stood on the other side of the road holding the lost necklace in his mouth. Jerry walked down the street and then crossed to the other side of the road, walking back and forth several times with his hand extended, hoping to make a good show of things. Gunter followed for a moment before sitting and cocking his head to the side as if trying to decide if Jerry had officially lost his mind. After a few moments had passed, Jerry pulled out his pocketknife and cellphone and dropped to his knees.

Susie now stood across from him on the other side of the road. "Did you find something?"

"I think so." Even though he doubted she could see him, Jerry plunged the knife into the dirt and pretended to dig. He motioned to Gunter, who walked to where Jerry crouched. The dog was still holding the dirty necklace between his teeth. Jerry took it from him. He was just getting ready to thrust it into the air and proclaim his victory when he decided he'd better have a look to make sure it was in fact the one Susie had lost.

Jerry cleared the dirt away with his fingernail

and pried the locket open. As he looked at the tiny photo, his mouth went dry. Trying his best to keep his emotions in check, he stood and was in the middle of the road before realizing he'd forgotten to look for cars. He did so now and gave thanks for the lack of traffic. His hands were trembling by the time he reached Susie and handed her the necklace.

"I can't believe you found it after all this time." She opened it and looked at the photo, and hugged it to her chest. Frowning, she ran a hand through her dark hair as she met Jerry's gaze. "There's something else I didn't tell anyone."

"Something about that night?"

She nodded. "I had seen the man before. He was in the restaurant. He was sitting at another table and asked to be moved to my section. When I asked him why, he said he had a thing for redheads."

All the things that had been bugging him fell into place. It was dark during the altercation, which Susie claimed to have only lasted a few seconds before she hit him with the pepper spray, yet Susie had said the man had brown eyes. Even though the man would have towered over her, she knew him to have a bald spot on the top of his head. Still, Jerry had a lot more questions. Did he engage her in conversation? Did she maybe flirt a little extra in hopes of getting a better tip? Not that he would judge her for it; servers did it all the time. He just wanted to know if she'd gotten a feel for the guy's mindset. The problem was he didn't want to scare her off before bringing in reinforcements. He decided to ask the safest question. "Is that why you colored your hair?"

"Yes. The police didn't catch the guy. I thought he might still be out there."

Jerry took a chance. "I have some friends that would be interested in talking with you. Is it okay if I give them a call?"

"I've already talked to the police. I'm not sure they even believed me."

"My friends will believe you."

Susie clutched the necklace. "Will you be there?"

Jerry smiled. "I wouldn't miss it for the world."

Chapter Three

Though Susie had invited him up to her apartment, Jerry declined. The last thing he wanted was to do anything to jeopardize the case. Nor did he wish to leave their star witness alone without protection, which was why he'd left Gunter to guard the woman while he went back to retrieve his Durango, which he currently sat in waiting for Fred and Barney to arrive. Though the duo hadn't told him their precise location, Jerry knew they hadn't been too far away, as they'd promised to be there within the hour. Of course, that may have been because though Jerry had told them he'd gotten a big break in the case, he'd refused to tell them the details. Nor had he called anyone else to fill them in and further asked Susie to refrain from speaking of the case until after she spoke to his friends.

A black town car rounded the corner, came alongside him, and lowered the driver's side window. Fred leveled a look at him. "I thought we held the market on cloak and dagger."

Though Jerry felt he could trust the men, he also knew Fabel had a way of finding things out. While the man had promised to allow Jerry to do his thing, he didn't doubt the man was tracking his every move. If Fabel were to find out there was someone who could identify the man who'd killed his sister, he might decide to terminate their little agreement. "Some things are best not talked about over the phone."

"You know we are the ones listening, right?"

Jerry smiled. "I do now."

The corners of the man's mouth lifted ever so slightly. "So what do you have, and who are you trying to keep it from?"

"Fabel."

Fred's forehead creased. "You've got Fabel? I thought he promised to back off."

"I haven't seen Mario Fabel, but the man seems to have a way of collecting information he shouldn't have. I doubt that would change if the information were in his backyard."

Fred leaned in closer. "I'm listening."

"First, I have some conditions."

Fred turned to Barney. "The man wants to play on our playground but insists on making up his own rules." He turned his attention back to Jerry. "This better be good."

"Better than good. What if I told you I have someone who can identify the Hash Mark Killer."

Fred shook his head. "I'd say that's good."

"Good enough to get my witness some protection

until we nail the guy?"

"Is this the waitress you were telling me about?"

"I need your word first, and then I'll talk."

"If this girl's the real deal, we'll take care of her."

"She's the real deal. I knew it even before she told me."

"Where is she now?"

"Upstairs in her apartment."

"If you're so worried about her, why did you leave her alone?"

Jerry smiled. "I never said she was alone."

"She got a roommate?"

"Nope. A ninety-pound police dog."

"I thought you said he's always with you."

"He is."

"But you just said…"

Jerry's smile widened. "Don't try to figure it out. It will drive you mad."

"Is she willing to talk to us?"

"Yes, but I didn't fill her in on the details. She's tough, but she had a bad scare. I didn't want to give her time to reconsider or talk to anyone who could convince her not to cooperate. As far as she knows, I'm bringing in some friends to help catch the guy who tried to abduct her."

Fred nodded. "Smart. So where do you want to do this?"

"Not here. I don't want anything that can be talked about if anyone comes snooping."

Fred turned to Barney. "Make a call and get us a room. No windows."

He turned back to Jerry. "Give us about thirty minutes to get everything ready and bring the girl. I'll text you the address as soon as I get it."

***

Jerry accompanied Susie to a government building in the heart of Westerly, not far from where the woman worked. Fred and Barney were waiting outside the room when they stepped off the elevator.

"Susie Richardson, meet Fred and Barney. Fred and Barney, meet Susie."

Susie snickered. "No, fair. I want a cool cartoon name too."

Jerry tried his best to keep from laughing as Fred extended his hand to Susie. "Sorry to disappoint, but those are our real names."

Susie blushed. "I'm sorry. I thought…"

Fred brushed her off. "No worries, we get it all the time."

"I guess I wasn't what you expected."

The lines between Fred's brows deepened. "What makes you say that?"

"Because you haven't stopped frowning since I stepped off the elevator." She shrugged. "It's what I do, study faces."

Fred worked to get rid of the lines. "You seem to be very good at it. No, I don't have a problem with you. I was just under the impression that you were a redhead."

"Dye job. I did it myself." Susie tugged at her hair and beamed. "You'd never know the carpet doesn't match the drapes."

Barney laughed and covered it with a cough.

The door to the room opened, and a man with a long wand exited and gave them the thumbs-up sign. "Clean as a whistle."

Susie turned toward Jerry and frowned. "Was he looking for bugs?"

Fred answered for him. "You're very astute, Ms. Richardson. I'm assuming that is why you are still alive."

Susie looked at Jerry once more. "What's he talking about."

Jerry cupped her elbow and led her into the room. "I'd prefer we talk in here."

Jerry led the way to the table and skirted around to the other side so he was facing the door. Susie took a seat, and Jerry sat beside her. He pushed the chair beside him out of the way. Gunter plopped down on the floor beside him as Fred took a chair on the opposite side of the table closest to the door. Barney busied himself with hooking up a recording device. A moment later, a woman entered. Wearing a pencil skirt and matching jacket, she took a seat in the corner of the room and pulled out a tablet and pen.

Jerry jutted his chin toward the woman. "Who's

she?"

Barney took a seat next to Fred. "Mrs. Taylor is one of ours and can be fully trusted. She will be taking notes while the machine records."

Susie shifted in her chair. "This seems like a lot of trouble for a failed abduction."

Fred smiled a disarming smile. When he spoke, his tone was just as charming. "No need to worry yourself. We just want to make sure we get everything we can, so that when we catch this guy, we have everything we need to put him away. What say we begin with you telling us your name?"

"You already know my name."

Barney paused the recorder. "We need it for the official record."

Jerry had to agree with Fred. The woman's sass was probably what kept her alive. "You're probably going to get sick of repeating yourself, but I assure you the questions are necessary."

Fred nodded to Barney, who restarted the machine, then focused on Susie. "For the record, what is your name?"

"Rebecca Sue Richardson. My friends call me Susie."

"Your age? For the record," Fred added when she balked.

"Twenty-three."

"And you live here in Westerly, Rhode Island?"

"Just for the summer. I'll be heading back to

Westwood next week."

"Westwood; that would be in?"

"Massachusetts. It's where I go to college."

Jerry rolled his neck. Here he was trying to keep her away from Fabel, and she lived in his backyard. *Easy does it, McNeal. There are plenty of colleges around. It won't be difficult for her to switch.* He glanced at Susie. "Ever thought about switching schools?"

"You're getting ahead of yourself, McNeal," Fred warned.

"Just covering all the bases."

Susie shook her head. "Yeah, well, I'm a year into a two-year program. I'm not starting over. I've got big plans. Next year, I graduate and get my license, and in two more years, I hope to have my own business."

Fred looked over the table and smiled. "What business is that?"

"I'm going to own my own mortuary." The smile left Fred's face as Barney's eyes bugged.

Susie laughed a hearty laugh. "Gets them every time."

Fred recovered. "I dare say when you said you study faces and color your own hair, I did expect you to say you were going to beauty college."

Susie shrugged. "Nah, I couldn't make it as a beautician. Too peopley. Drives me nuts just to get my hair done. You couldn't pay me to do hair on a live person. I give those ladies who do it major props. I swear everyone who steps into a hair salon acts as if they booked a session with their personal therapist. No, siree, not for me. I like my work quiet, so I can hear myself think. That's why I prefer working with the dead. They don't talk back."

That's what you think, lady. Jerry bit his tongue to keep from voicing his opinion out loud.

"Seems as if you and Mr. McNeal have a lot in common," Fred offered.

Susie turned in her chair. "Really? Why's that?"

Jerry glared at Fred. He didn't like talking about his gift unless it was his idea.

Fred took the look as it was intended and reeled in the conversation. "I was merely making an observation that, like you, Mr. McNeal is not much of a people person. If you would please continue."

"Okay, so I grew up in Maine. Where doesn't matter because I haven't been home in years. My mom and stepdad moved to Texas because they were tired of the cold. I went in the Army right out of high school. Stayed in two years and got out. Before you ask, I had it planned. Serve long enough to qualify for a GI bill and use that to pay for mortuary school."

Fred shook his head. "I don't believe I've ever heard of a woman mortician."

"There are plenty out there."

"Still, I must ask why?" Fred pressed.

Jerry had to admit he was curious as well.

"Because the dead don't complain."

Jerry laughed, and Gunter growled. Jerry recovered and moved his leg next to the dog in an effort to soothe him. He ran a hand over his head before speaking. "We seem to have gotten off subject. Can you please tell them what you told me about the night you were attacked?"

"It was after my shift. The guy was hiding near the tree by the park. He brought his hand up like he was going to cover my mouth. Only I was ready for him. I screamed, elbowed him in the gut, and blasted his face with pepper spray. Then I ran to the house down the street."

Jerry felt a tingle on the back of his neck. "You said you were ready for him."

"I had pepper spray in my hand. I always carry it when I'm walking home. But I'd had a feeling that something bad was going to happen all day." She looked at Jerry. "It's why I took my mom's ring off the chain."

Don't get sidetracked, McNeal. Jerry rolled his neck and continued with the questioning. "Did you know the man?"

"I told you I…"

Jerry cut her off. "For the record."

"No. I didn't know him. But I'd seen him earlier. I was at work, and he asked to be moved to my table."

"You're a waitress. Is that correct?"

"Yes."

"Do you know why the man asked to be moved?"

"He said he had a thing for redheads."

Fred picked up the questioning. "Lucky you. A man with a thing for redheads. A man likes a woman enough he's sure to leave a sizable tip. Did you do anything to fuel his fire?"

Susie shifted in her seat. It was the first time she seemed truly uncomfortable with the questions.

"No one is trying to accuse you of anything. My sister was a waitress. I know the things that can be done to earn a larger tip. A little cleavage here, a smile there." It wasn't the first time Jerry had used his nonexistent sister to get someone to talk. He looked at Fred, who knew good and well Jerry didn't have a sister. The man gave the slightest nod. A silent understanding that said it was better to get everything out in the open now so there were no surprises later on.

Susie pulled at her shirt. "I didn't show any cleavage. Not that I wouldn't if I had any to show. But as you can see, that's not the case. I smiled at the guy, but nothing I don't do to anyone else. It was busy, so I didn't have time to talk to him."

Jerry decided to push the issue. "But you spoke to him long enough for him to let you know he liked redheads."

Fred jumped in. "Did he say anything else?"

Susie shook her head. "No, the guy just told me what he wanted to eat – a small cheese pizza and a hard lemonade. And to thank me for being so nice to him. Which was plain weird, as I hadn't done anything more than take his order and check on him a couple of times."

"So nothing that could have been construed as flirting?"

"If he thought I was flirting with him, he was even more wack than I thought."

Fred jotted something on the paper in front of him. "What did the guy look like?"

"He was about six foot, brown hair, balding at the crown. Brown eyes."

Fred wrote down the description and tapped his pen on the table. "For a girl who takes pride in studying faces, you're not giving us much to help find this guy. My guess is you didn't get a good enough look at him to point him out in a lineup."

Susie glared at Fred. "The reason I can't give you more is there is nothing to give. There was nothing that set him apart. His eyes were evenly spaced. His lips perfectly shaped. His ears sat evenly on his head. His hair was perfectly combed, eyebrows evenly shaped. I mean, he just blended in with everyone around him."

Fred sighed. "Then you couldn't pick him out."

"Sure, I could."

"But you just said…"

"I said there were no distinguishing marks that would help you find the guy. But his lack of imperfections is exactly why I could pick him out if you put him in a room full of other guys."

Fred looked at Barney, who nodded his approval.

Susie looked between the three of them and focused on Jerry. "I don't know what everyone is so happy about. It's not like I helped you find the guy."

Jerry sighed. "I think we should tell her."

Fred's face remained stoic. "That wasn't part of the deal."

"She'll find out soon enough."

Susie slammed her fist on the table. "What deal? What aren't you telling me?"

Gunter barked, scrambling out from under the table, his nails clicking on the tiled floor. Moving next to Jerry, he growled a throaty growl as if trying to decide who he was supposed to be guarding against.

Jerry kept his voice even. "You said you'd keep her safe."

"Guys?"

Jerry held up a hand to silence her. "Part of keeping her safe is letting her know what we are keeping her safe from."

Susie pushed back from her chair. "Guys? You really need to focus here."

Come on, Susie, I'm trying to help. Jerry started to tell Susie to stop interrupting when he saw her eyes were wide with fear. He followed her gaze and realized she was looking right at Gunter. Jerry swallowed and looked at both Fred and Barney, neither of which showed any sign of seeing the ghostly K-9. Jerry placed his palms together and brought them to his lips. He smiled at Susie as another piece of the puzzle fell into place.

Chapter Four

Jerry held his hands rigid as he patted his right hand on top of the finger of his left, essentially calling a time out. Jerry caught Fred's attention and nodded toward Susie. "We need to take a break."

Seeing Susie's wide-eyed expression, Fred motioned for Barney to turn off the machine and then did a finger wag, letting Mrs. Taylor know it was time for her to leave.

He waited until the woman had left the room before turning his attention to Susie. "Are you alright, Ms. Richardson?"

"No, I'm not alright. I want to know what's going on. What are you keeping from me, and most of all, how did that dog get in here?"

Barney's eyes sprang open as Fred's mouth dropped. Recovering, Fred peered over the table and then back at Susie. "You mean you can see it?"

"Of course I can see him. He's standing right there." She pointed directly at Gunter. "Is this some kind of test to see if I can identify the man?"

"If you can give us a moment, Susie, I need to speak with Fred." Jerry did a head jerk and walked to the other side of the room. Gunter followed and sat leaning against Jerry's leg. Fred took his time joining them. Once there, he didn't wait to see what Jerry had to say. "Can she really see the dog?"

Jerry crossed his arms. "I didn't coax her, if that's what you're asking."

"Why now? I'm assuming he's been with you all along. If she was going to see him, wouldn't she have seen him earlier?"

Jerry shrugged. "I don't know. I know she felt him earlier. We were walking, Gunter got close, and she moved to the opposite side of the sidewalk. She also made a comment about feeling that something was going to happen. My gut tells me she has psychic abilities that were neither condoned nor condemned when she was young. It got a little heated earlier, and Gunter picked up on that enough that his energy was more pronounced. In turn, Susie was able to see him."

At hearing his name, Gunter tilted his head, his long ears pointing toward the others.

Fred looked over at Susie. The girl was chatting with Barney and appeared somewhat calmer than before. "So this psychic thing. It's just lying there dormant until something triggers it?"

"More or less. I would have to talk with her more to see. But it explains what pulled me here."

"I'm not following."

"Patti, Rita, and the others seem to have a

connection. I don't know what it is, unless it's because they all were killed by the same man. While he obviously didn't kill Susie, he tried."

"So you think that is the connection or what brought you here?"

"Unless…what if it's more convoluted than that?"

Fred pressed his backside against the table. "Float your theory, McNeal."

"Patti knew I would be going to see Ashley. That is why she told me to take Max's call. All of the women know there are others. They haven't referred to them by name, but they know. That's why they each have used the word 'us.' Help 'us,' Jerry. You're the only one."

Fred blew a low whistle. "That's a load to carry."

Jerry chuckled. "Tell me about it. Anyway, if they knew about each other, maybe they know about Susie and know she is the one person who can identify the killer. Make sense?"

"No more sense than your being able to talk to ghosts or communicate with a ghost dog. Which means you're probably right." Fred sighed. "So, you think we need to bring her into the loop?"

Jerry cocked an eyebrow. "You're kidding, right? I don't think we have any other choice. If she is as tied to the others as we think, we will need her. I also think it will help keep her safe. If she does have the gift, she needs to know. That way, she won't blow it off. Even if the killer never finds her, it could save her life another day."

"You may not understand this stuff, but you're pretty darn good at figuring it out." Fred pushed off the table. "I'm sure glad you're on our team."

Jerry rocked back on his heels. "Who said anything about me being on your team?"

Fred smiled. "You didn't call your buddy Seltzer. You called us. That tells me you weighed your options and decided we were the best fit. This is how it works, McNeal. You do your thing, and when you need us, we are there."

Jerry rolled his neck. While he was warming to the idea, he wasn't quite ready to commit.

Fred took his lack of refusal as a positive sign as he continued to push. "Here's the deal. You know you are one of us, and we know you are one of us. You just need to say the words to make it official."

"Why do I have to make it official? Why can't I just keep on doing what I'm doing?"

"Because there may come an occasion where we would ask you to check into some things we are working on. Things we can't share unless we know you are one of us."

"Isn't that what I will be doing in Mystic?"

The smile disappeared from Fred's face. "Mystic's different."

"How so?"

"Mystic is personal. Listen, what do you say we

get this tied up so you can get to it?" Fred started toward the other side of the room, and Jerry followed. Fred reached over Barney, intending to start the recorder.

Jerry took hold of his arm and leveled a look at the man. "Leave it off."

Fred held his gaze for a full beat before pulling his hand back.

Satisfied this would remain off the record, Jerry started the conversation. "What we are about to discuss must not leave this room. All of it."

Susie looked at each man in turn then nodded her agreement.

"Fred, you've got the floor." Jerry leaned back in his seat. Gunter sat next to him, resting his chin on Jerry's thigh.

Fred stood and walked about the room as he spoke. "We believe the man who tried to abduct you to be a man known only as the Hash Mark Killer."

Jerry struggled to keep from smiling. They could have easily gone with the Redhead Killer or used any number of titles to identify the man.

Susie sucked in her breath. "Killer?"

Fred shook his head. "That's right. Four women that we know of. We feel certain there are more victims."

"Wait? You think that jerk aimed to kill me?"

Fred gripped the back of a chair and stared across the table. The intensity of the look stripped

Jerry from any pride he'd felt in giving the killer his moniker. Fred nodded. "Among other things. The man is brutal in his attacks."

"How can you be sure it's the same guy?"

Because the other victims told me. Jerry held his breath, half expecting Fred to call him out. Jerry planned to tell her himself, but not yet – not after just learning of her near miss with a serial killer.

Fred let go of the chair and began pacing once more. "Because all of his victims were redheads."

Susie ran her hand through her dark hair. "That doesn't seem like a lot to go on."

"It's not. But it's all we have at the moment. That and you."

Understanding washed over the girl's face as she slowly nodded her head. "Because I can identify him?"

"Yes, which is why Mr. McNeal has asked that we move you into protective custody until after we catch this guy."

"How long will that be?"

Fred sighed. "That is a question I don't have an answer to. It could be days, weeks, or even years. We have Mr. McNeal on the case, so I expect to find the man sooner than later."

Jerry expected her to ask what made him so special. Instead, she answered with a single word.

"No." It was a simple answer said with conviction.

*Of all the stubborn...*Jerry pushed his chair back and pivoted, facing the woman. Instantly, Gunter was on his feet, barking.

Susie sucked in a breath, but Fred and Barney showed no sign they'd heard the dog.

Jerry raised a hand to silence the barking, saw Susie looking, and brushed the hand over his head. "What do you mean no? It's the only way to keep you safe."

"Then find another way. I'm not going to quit school, nor will I allow some psychopath to derail a career plan I put together before I even finished high school. You guys are smart. You'll have to come up with a different solution."

Jerry crossed his arms in front of him. "There are no other solutions. This guy finds out you are alive, and you're as good as dead."

Susie narrowed her eyes. "I'll get a gun. I know how to use one. Besides, I've taken care of myself until now."

Jerry took hold of her arm, and she glared at him. He let go, lifting his hands for her to see. "If you don't let us protect you, you'll die. You know how you said you knew something bad would happen? That was intuition. I have it too. Only mine is much stronger than yours because I use it every day. It's part of me and what led me to you." Jerry splayed his fingers and circled the room with his arms. "My meeting you wasn't random. My intuition guided me here to help protect you, and I know with utmost certainty if you don't listen, you will die."

"By this Hash Mark Killer guy?"

Jerry ran a hand over his head. "Him or someone who wants to find him as much as we do."

"Someone who?"

"Don't say it," Fred warned.

Undeterred, Jerry pressed on. "Mario Fabel. His sister is one of the women who we know to have been killed by this guy."

Fred slammed a chair against the wall, and Gunter growled as Fred shook his finger at Jerry. "You can't go around slandering people like that."

Jerry shrugged off his words. "I'm not saying anything that isn't true. Mario Fabel wants to find the killer as much as we do. Only if Fabel finds him before we do, he will administer his own justice."

Susie shrugged her indifference. "What's wrong with that?"

"Because I promised Patti O'Conner, Ashley Fabel, Rita Wadsworth, and Rosie Freeman that I would see the man brought to justice. I promised they would see the man convicted of his crimes."

Susie's brow furrowed. "I thought you said I am the only witness."

"We said you are the only living witness. Remember that gift I told you about?" Jerry rolled his neck, watching as she absorbed his words.

Susie's eyes darted from Jerry to the others and

back again. "Are you telling me you can talk to ghosts?"

"They prefer to be called spirits."

Fred cleared his throat.

Jerry smiled. "It's true."

That Susie didn't immediately tell him he was crazy was a good sign. Once again, Jerry and the others gave her time to process what she'd heard. Her eyes widened. "The dog?!"

Jerry nodded.

"I thought I saw a dog when we were walking, and I didn't want you to think I was a kook. Then when he just showed up in the room, I was like, how could I not have seen him? Then he started barking, and you were the only one who reacted." She looked at the others. "You can't see him."

Fred shook his head. "Not for lack of trying, though."

Go ahead and ask, McNeal. You know you're dying to know. "Have you always been able to see spirits?"

Susie answered without hesitation. "Pretty much. But sometimes it is more of a mist or a feeling that lets me know something is there. Not dogs, though. That was pretty cool. I didn't know they even existed. Most of the time, the spirits are not as vivid as the dog was. This is a first for me."

"So you're like Jerry?"

Susie looked at Fred and shook her head. "No. I

can see them, but I've never talked to them – not and have them answer. I honestly didn't know it was possible. I guess I owe Jennifer Love Hewitt an apology."

Jerry shook his head. "No, you don't. I doubt she can really talk to ghosts. Is that why you picked mortuary school?"

"No. Maybe. Who knows." She shrugged. "I picked it because it sounded cool, and there's good money in it."

Barney, who'd been quiet through the whole exchange, cleared his throat and raised his hand, speaking only when he had everyone's attention. "If we're done with the ghost stories, I have a suggestion. What if we assign an agent to shadow Susie?"

Fred nodded his agreement. "That could work."

Jerry looked at Susie, whose face told him she was considering it.

Barney pushed forward. "We get someone who blends in and set them up in the same classes. How big is your apartment?"

Susie sighed. "I live in the dorm."

"Not anymore, you don't. We'll get you an apartment near the college. Someplace we can control. The only stipulation is you must be accompanied anytime you go out. You want to go on a date, make it a double."

Susie frowned. "Who's paying for this

apartment?"

"They are." Jerry looked to the others, who shook their head in agreement.

A sly smile crossed Susie's lips. "For the whole year. Even if you catch the guy right away, I don't want to have to move again in the middle of the school year."

Fred looked down his nose at her. "Anything else?"

"You pay all utilities. Including cable – with premium channels." She winked. "My GI bill only goes so far."

Fred sat back in his chair. Jerry could tell the man was enjoying the exchange. "Is that all?"

"This agent you have shadowing me pays for her own food."

Jerry looked at Fred. "I think we can get your food covered as well. What do you think, Fred?"

Fred closed his eyes. When he reopened them, he smiled a genuine smile. "What do I think? I think this lady is missing her true calling. She's one shrewd negotiator."

Jerry drummed his fingers on the table. "One more thing. I'm going to set you up to talk to a friend of mine who can help you further enhance your psychic abilities."

Susie beamed and nodded her consent.

Jerry relaxed. For the first time since arriving in town, the crawling sensation, along with the pull that had brought him here, was gone.

Chapter Five

Jerry turned on the ignition and scrolled through his cell phone, checking for messages.

Gunter woofed and Jerry looked to see Fred hurrying toward them. Jerry placed the cell in the cup holder.

Gunter circled two tight circles in the passenger seat then sat, watching Fred's approach.

Fred placed his hand on the car door as if doing so would prevent Jerry from leaving. "Glad I caught you. I presume you're heading to Mystic."

You already know the answer to that. "That's the plan."

"Where are you staying?"

Jerry shrugged. "I thought I would do what I always do and figure that out when I got there."

Fred sighed. "It's tourist season. Unless you want to sleep in your vehicle, take this."

Jerry took the paper Fred offered. "What's this?"

"The address to a studio apartment on Pearl Street. It's a nice place if you don't mind stairs."

"Whose place?"

"It belongs to my sister and her husband."

"The one with the kid?"

"That's the one."

Jerry rolled his neck.

Fred dangled a key chain hosting a single key in front of him. "Don't worry, McNeal, she won't bother you. She wants this solved as much as I do. She knows what you do, to a point, and knows better than to interfere."

Jerry sighed and reached for the key. "This house, is it where the kid disappeared from?"

"No." Fred handed him a manilla envelope. "This has everything you need, including a transcript from the lead suspect's interrogation. You got a computer?"

"Yes." Jerry sighed. *Not that I ever use it.*

Fred ignored the sigh and handed him a thumb drive. "Here's the video of the interrogation. If you need anything, I'll be nearby."

Jerry opened the envelope, dropped the thumb drive inside, and tucked it between the seat and the console. "How nearby?"

"I'll be in the area for the next few days."

"I prefer to work alone." Gunter grumbled-growled his displeasure, and Jerry corrected himself. "We…me and the dog. Gunter didn't like that I'd left him out."

Fred laughed a hearty laugh. "Man, I thought getting chastised by my wife was bad enough."

Jerry joined in on the chuckle. "He doesn't like

to be left out of the mix."

Fred used his finger to wipe the corner of his eye. "About the dog. I trust you to clean up after him if he makes a mess."

Jerry smiled. "Your sister won't even know he's there."

Fred pointed to the street. "You can plug the address into the navigator if you want. She'll probably take you down I95." He pointed up the road. "If it were me, I'd go straight here and follow US-1 South straight into Mystic so you can get a feel for the town and see if anything calls to you. After you cross over the drawbridge, Pearl Street will be a couple streets up on your right. And, McNeal, I want you to nail this guy."

"If he is guilty."

Fred's ears turned pink. "Oh, he's guilty alright."

"I'll look into it." Even though he'd yet to look at a single shred of evidence, Jerry wasn't convinced. Fred had the resources to find out what the man had for lunch on any given day of the week. If the guy had perpetrated the crime, the man would have nailed his groin to the wall by now. The fact that Fred was still standing there made Jerry wonder if Fred had read his mind. Jerry placed his hands on the wheel. "Is there anything else?"

Fred kicked at the sidewalk with the toe of his shoe for a solid minute before speaking. "My sister knows you are psychic, and I may have told her you have a ghost dog that you can communicate with. She knows you are coming to town, but I didn't tell her why."

Jerry smiled. "And you don't want me to tell her I can speak to all spirits because she won't believe me."

Fred shook his head. "No, I didn't tell her because I'm afraid she will believe you."

"You don't want her to know if her daughter has a message for her?"

"No." Fred grimaced. "I don't know. I guess it depends on the message. Let's just keep that bit of information to ourselves for now."

Something was eating at the man. "Just say what's on your mind, Fred."

"I just don't want to get her hopes up any more than they are."

Jerry looked at Gunter before speaking. "You're not saying your sister thinks we will find her alive, are you?"

Fred sighed. "Sarah knows better than that – at least I think so. But if she knows you can talk to ghosts and my niece doesn't appear, show herself, materialize, or whatever it's called, Sarah will be even more devastated. She already thinks she let the girl down by not keeping a closer eye on her."

"Understood. If I get a lead on anything, I'll bring it to you first."

Jerry pulled away from the curb the second Fred cleared the front. As he drove, he thought about what Fred had said about his sister blaming herself for her daughter's disappearance. He thought back to the day he and Gunter had found Holly nestled within the snow-covered clutch of trees. Though she'd been trapped and fearful for her life, her thoughts had been mostly of her daughter. He remembered Holly's anguish at having let the child down and wondered what it would feel like to love someone so much that you'd do anything to protect them. He further wondered if he would ever find out what it was like to be a parent.

Gunter groaned and placed his head on the console. Not for the first time, Jerry debated the benefits of ordering the dog to stay out of his head. "You're a pain in the …"

Jerry turned his attention to the screen as the Uconnect announced a call from Max. "Hey, kiddo, what's up?"

"Nothing. I just kind of missed you. It's alright that I called even if I don't need anything, isn't it? I wanted to call before but didn't want to be a bother."

"Max, you could never be a bother. If you want to call, then call."

"Even if it's only to tell you I've got nothing to say?"

Gunter looked at the dash and wagged his tail.

Jerry laughed. "Especially if you have nothing to

say. Then I won't have anything to worry about."

"You mean you worry about me?"

"Of course I do. I'd do anything to make sure you are safe." As the words came out of his mouth, he realized they were true.

Gunter barked.

"Hi, Gunter. I miss you too."

Instantly, giggles floated through the speakers of the dash. "Jerry! Gunter's here. He's licking my face!"

Jerry looked at the passenger seat. Empty. *Well, what do you know about that?* Something about him going to see Max warmed his heart. "I guess he missed you too. Hey, I wanted to tell you that you got another one."

"Another one what?" she asked between giggles.

"That number you keyed on – 207, it was right."

"It was?"

"Yes. It was the number to my hotel room this past week. By you telling me to be careful, I was able to avoid a situation." Jerry didn't want to worry her, so he stopped short of telling her the full details. "I thought you'd be pleased to know."

"I am. Sort of. It's just that I don't think that's it."

"What do you mean? I thought you keyed on the number 207."

"I did, but you said you'd already left."

"Yes, I left this morning." *Wow, that was this morning. It feels like a week ago.*

"That's enough, Gunter. Go back to Jerry."

Jerry could hear the concern in her voice. He saw a shadow and looked to see Gunter sitting in the seat beside him. The dog's tongue hung from his mouth as he smiled a K-9 smile.

"What is it, Max?"

"I don't know. There is still something with that number."

"What kind of something?"

"Sadness. Fear. I'm not sure, but I don't like it."

"Don't worry, Max. I'll keep an eye out." *Think, Jerry, change the subject.* "So how are things in Michigan? Anything new?"

Max's voice instantly brightened. "Is there ever. We bought the house."

"Which house?"

"The one we are in. Mom told Carrie about the money – she didn't tell her how much. Just that we got a reward. Don't get mad – Carrie won't tell anyone!"

"I'm not mad, Max. It is you guys' money. I just don't want anyone to take advantage of you or swindle you out of it."

"Carrie isn't like that. She told Mom we could buy the house and even told her she'd been keeping all the rent money Mom had paid in a savings account for her. She was going to surprise Mom one day by telling her she'd paid enough money to buy the house. She said she wasn't going to charge much since it was her grandmother's house and already paid for. Anyway, she told Mom that she would use the rent payments as a down payment. We still have plenty of money left."

Jerry wished he'd gotten a chance to meet Carrie when he'd gone to Michigan. She sounded like a lovely lady and a true friend to Max and April. "That's wonderful, Max."

"I know. Mom and I have already started stripping the wallpaper off the walls in the living room. Mom insisted on doing that room first since it is the one everyone sees when they come over. Mom is looking for a handyman to do some of the big stuff, and I get to pick out new furniture for my bedroom and new bedding as soon as I figure out what I want."

As Max continued to talk about what she wanted for her room, Jerry felt a tinge of regret he wasn't in a position to help. He had the know-how, as he'd remodeled his garage apartment in Pennsylvania and did a partial remodel on Savannah and Alex's bathroom in Tennessee. Jerry pulled his hand from the steering wheel and flexed his fingers, recalling his moment of anger when he'd punched the mirror. *A costly mistake.*

"You think so?"

Jerry realized he had gotten caught up in his own thoughts. "What?"

"I said I hoped Momma would redo the kitchen,

and you said it would be a costly mistake."

No, I thought it. It dawned on Jerry he had never told Max to stay out of his head. He started to, then decided against it. Max had saved his behind too many times to chance it. Still, he thought it might be good to figure out how to set boundaries. "It could be costly if it's not done right. Make sure to tell your mom to hire a carpenter with business insurance."

"Okay, I'll tell her. Do you think you'll be able to find the little girl?"

She's doing it again. Not for the first time, Jerry admired the girl's psychic abilities. "I'm going to try my best."

"She's dead, isn't she?"

Don't sugarcoat it, Jerry. She will see right through it. "It's been a long time, Max. So my hunch is telling me that she is."

"Yeah, mine too."

"You've got a good record of reading the situation even before I know. I'll let you know if I need help."

"Cool. I like helping you."

"You should. You're quite good at it. And let's face it, you haven't been wrong yet."

"Except with 207."

"I didn't say you were wrong."

"No, I did. It just doesn't feel like I was."

"Maybe you weren't. I'll keep an eye out and let you know if I see it again." Jerry passed a small car dealership and started to see businesses and houses sprinkled here and there. “Good job, kiddo. You kept me company all the way to my destination.”

“Where are you?”

“Mystic, Connecticut.”

“Like in the movie?”

“I didn’t know there was a movie.”

“Yep. *Mystic Pizza*.”

“I’ll have to check it out.”

Max laughed. “I think it’s a chick flick.”

“Maybe I like chick flicks.” *Not likely*. Gunter sat up in the seat and stared out the window as they grew closer to town. “Okay, Max. It’s time for me to do my thing. Are you good, kiddo?”

“Yep, I’m good. Thanks for talking to me, Jerry.”

“Anytime, Max. And I really do mean that.” Jerry pressed to end the call and looked over at Gunter. “You know that was a pretty cool trick. I’m glad you got to see Max. I have to admit I’m a wee bit jealous over that one. I wish I could beam myself to different places. It would sure as heck beat all this driving.”

Gunter answered by sticking his head through the window glass.

A white building on the right caught his eye. Jerry read the sign as he slowed for traffic stopped at the light. The Inn at Mystic. To the left was an ancient graveyard that butted up against the water. The light turned green, and he followed the line of traffic into town.

He passed the firehouse on the left and followed the curve to the left at the church to continue on US-1. The town was filling in, with more and more houses and a small red brick post office with on-street parking. Traffic slowed on the two-lane road before coming to a complete stop. He noted the lack of traffic heading in the opposite direction. *Great, there must be an accident.* He craned his neck and saw a bridge, then remembered Fred's mention of a drawbridge. *Cool.*

Jerry's mind traveled back to the firehouse he'd passed. "Hmm, I wonder what the town does if there is a fire emergency on the other side when the bridge is up? Do you think maybe there's another firehouse that services the other side of town?"

Gunter didn't answer.

Jerry looked in the rearview mirror to see what had gotten the dog's attention and smiled. A bright red Mini Cooper convertible idled directly behind them. In the passenger seat sat a beautiful snow-white boxer. The blonde sitting in the driver's seat wasn't so bad either – at least what he could see of her beneath the oversized sunglasses and hat. That the dog had captured Gunter's full attention led Jerry to believe it was also a female. "Easy there, Romeo. We have a job to do. I'm going to need your full attention."

Gunter pulled his head back through the glass

and licked his lips.

Jerry noted the Whaler's Inn on the left, a stately establishment that took up a whole block and included a raw bar restaurant. Directly across the street was what looked to be an upscale sit-down restaurant. A grey building shaped like a lighthouse sat up on the left and was too far away to make out the sign. The light turned green, cars began to trickle through from the other side, and the lane he was in began to inch forward. He noted a toy shop on the left at the foot of the bridge and instantly thought of Max. He made a mental note to stop in before leaving town and find something special to send to her. When he looked again, he saw that the building was not in fact a toy store but a clothing boutique.

That's odd. Why did I see it as a toy store?

The Mini sounded the horn, and Jerry realized he'd come to a complete stop while checking out the shop. Okay, so maybe it wasn't a toy store, but from the looks of the building, it had once served as a gas station. He inched forward onto the bridge and noted the rumble of the tires as he drove across the bridge grate. He tried to get a better look at the bridge, which looked as if it used concrete counterweights, and made another mental note to come back on foot to check it out.

The street on the other side of the bridge was lined with shops. Cars lined the street on both sides, and the town was bustling with what Jerry presumed were tourists.

He passed the turn onto Gravel Street and continued. He took the next right onto Pearl Street, which was even narrower than the street he was just on. Pearl Street allowed street parking on the right, all of which were filled. He passed several businesses before the street gave way to dual-sided parking in front of the houses that made up the remainder of the road. Jerry looked at the paper Fred had given him. It showed a picture of a yellow house. *The house is across from the church parking lot. The apartment is located in the detached garage in the back. Help yourself to the beer in the fridge.*

As Jerry inched down the street, he saw the house that matched the photo on the paper Fred had given him. The yard was meticulous with well-manicured shrubs and trees and nary a blade of grass out of place. As he turned in to the driveway, he saw Fred's car parked near the garage. Neither he nor Barney were anywhere in sight, but the hair on the back of his neck told him one or both were near.

Chapter Six

The apartment over the garage proved to be a mostly open concept room with a full bath and walk-in closet. The small kitchen area had high-end furnishings with a beachy motif perfectly in tune with a seaport town – especially since the theme was carried through with such attention to detail. It was easy to see the space had been blessed by a woman's touch or at the least someone with much more attention to detail than he possessed, as he would never have thought to use the knotted ropes to hold the curtains in place. To him, a curtain was either open or closed. It was as simple as that. Still, Jerry himself felt confident in picking furnishings that looked well when placed together. Of course, it was hard to screw up as long as you chose a white toilet to go with a white tub. His interior design imagination didn't go much beyond being able to successfully choose coordinating towels. Then again, everything went with white.

Jerry pulled several days' worth of clothes from his seabag, placing them in an empty drawer of the dresser. Somehow retrieving his clothes from a dresser drawer instead of a green canvas bag helped give him a sense of normalcy. He thought about the traffic coming into town and the walkability of the area, and pulled out his sneakers. Seeing them, he dug a bit deeper and hauled out a pair of shorts and his favorite running shirt as well.

Gunter stepped beside him, sniffed the shoes, and licked his lips.

Jerry laughed and shoved him out of the way. "No eating my shoes." The command was totally unnecessary as Gunter had never destroyed anything. Jerry opened the door to the closet, and Gunter hurried past, nose to the ground, exploring the small space as Jerry placed the seabag in the corner. He placed the gun bag on the top rack of the closet, shut the door, then went to the window and looked out.

Gunter barked a muffled bark. Jerry realized he'd shut the dog in the closet and turned from the window. Before he reached the door, Gunter pushed his head through. Jerry stopped, watching as the rest of the dog's body followed.

Jerry laughed. "You sure are something, dog."

Gunter didn't appear as impressed as he ignored Jerry and jumped onto the sofa. Jerry collected the envelope Fred had given him and was getting ready to join the dog on the couch and decided against it when the dog began to lick himself. He took the envelope to the narrow kitchen island that divided the room. Jerry pulled out a photo of the little girl and committed her face to memory. Brown hair, hazel eyes, dimples. A second photo showed a dime-size strawberry birthmark on the right side of her neck just below her ear. Jerry stared at the image for several moments, trying to get a reading. He got nothing. Not that it surprised him; his gift was more of a hands-on talent. Pictures and objects were more in Savannah's swim lane, though he had little doubt Max would be able to get a line on the girl.

Gunter had settled on the couch, sleeping with his head on his paws. Jerry held up the photo. "Yo, dog. Can you get a lead off of this?"

Gunter opened his eyes, then closed them once more.

So much for ghosts not sleeping. Jerry snapped a picture of the photo with his cellphone camera, set the photo aside, and picked up the next. A note was attached telling the man's name to be Nick Stringer. Age twenty-eight, the man in the photo had a buzz haircut, quarter-size gauges in his ears that stood out from his head, and a tattoo of a snake on his right forearm. A sticky note on the front of the photo stated *This is our guy*. Jerry removed the note and set both the note and detail page aside.

He lifted the next photo and studied the man for a moment – grey hair, thin lips and wide-spaced eyes. Jerry looked at the accompanying notes. Robert Pence, age sixty-eight. Pence, who had a history of indecent exposure to minors, was in the area at the time of the disappearance. Pence had a kidney stone on the day in question and spent most of the day and the better part of the night at Pequot Health Center in Groton. While Jerry hadn't personally had a kidney stone, he'd known people who had. He doubted the man would have been able to stand up straight, much less commit a crime.

He set the photo aside and moved to the next, again studying the man before reading the attached note. The image showed a Hispanic male who looked to be in his mid to late thirties. Jerry skimmed the attached notice. Carlos Santorini, age thirty-eight, was listed on the sex offender list. Carlos was vacationing in the area and had even disclosed his SO status when requesting the rental. While his vacation rental house was down the street from where the child went missing, Santorini and his wife were out of the area on the day in question. An additional note stated he and his wife had traveled to East Haddam, CT, and toured Gillette Castle. A charge on the wife's credit card and video footage of the restaurant where the couple dined gave the man a solid alibi. Jerry sat the photo on top of the other and returned to Nick's photo.

He pulled the sheet free and read. Nick Stringer, a handyman, was working at a nearby house at the time Angie went missing. The homeowner had left the house for over an hour around the time the child disappeared and therefore could not confirm Nick's alibi. Jerry skimmed the notes. While the homeowner described Nick as having long hair when he arrived at his house that morning, when the police showed up at Nick's house later that day to question him, his head was freshly buzzed. Fresh scratches were noted on Nick's arm just above his tattoo. Even though it had been raining, there was a record of him running his work truck through the Westerly Car Wash three times within a fifteen-minute period two hours after Angie disappeared. Nick's coveralls were discovered in the waste bin at the lot.

Jerry tapped his fingers on the counter. *Okay, a little peculiar, but it still doesn't convict the man.* "Maybe the guy has OCD."

Jerry pulled the thumb drive from his pocket, twirling it in his hand. He looked at his computer, debating whether or not to watch Nick's interview. He decided against it. At least for now. If there were anything on there that would have even hinted the guy had abducted the girl, Fred would have hauled him in a long time ago. No, Jerry would have better luck speaking with the man in person. A few minutes in proximity to the guy and he would know if he was involved in the girl's disappearance, although in a perfect world, he would go straight to the source. Jerry sighed. While he'd been seeing and speaking with ghosts since he was a little boy, he hadn't had many dealings with child spirits. It wasn't that they didn't exist. It was that they were less trusting, especially if they'd had a traumatic experience that involved a stranger.

Jerry rolled his neck. He took out his notebook and jotted down Nick's Lamphere Road address. Setting the photo on top of the others, he pushed from the chair. The moment he stood, Gunter jumped off the couch, the back half of his body wiggling from side to side in excited anticipation.

Jerry reached out a hand and gave him a firm pat. "What say you pay a visit to Mr. Stringer?"

Gunter barked and spun in eager circles. They were halfway down the stairs when Jerry saw Fred coming out the back door of the house, walking with the determined stride of a man on a mission.

Fred bypassed his Town Car and made a beeline to Jerry. "What do you think?"

Jerry knew what the guy wanted – Nick's head on a silver platter. But Jerry wasn't prepared to give it to him, not until he was sure the guy played a part in Angie's disappearance. "It's a nice apartment."

Fred narrowed his eyes. "That's not what I meant, and you know it. I'm talking about Nick. He's our guy, right?"

Jerry held his ground as Gunter stood at his side, intently watching the exchange. "It's too early to tell."

Fred's nostrils flared. "What do you mean too

early to tell? The guy's a freakshow."

Jerry rolled his neck. "Just what I said. It is too early to tell. Just because the guy has tats and gauges doesn't mean he's your guy."

"Of course he's our guy. You saw the deposition. The guy's guilty as sin. With your track record, the judge will listen. It's an open and shut case."

Jerry planted his feet. "I didn't see it. Besides, this is not an open and shut case, and you know it. If it was, you wouldn't need my help nailing the man."

Fred's ears turned a brilliant shade of pink. "What do you mean you didn't see it? You must have at least seen a portion of it. You've been up there for over an hour."

Jerry turned toward the stairs.

Fred grabbed him by the arm, and Gunter growled.

Jerry quickly gave the signal telling the dog to stand down. Gunter took a step back, but his teeth were bared, showing he was ready if Jerry should change his mind. Jerry looked Fred in the eye and kept his voice even. "I know you can't see the dog, but he is not very happy that you have your hand on me. The only reason you're not already on the ground is he thinks you are one of the good guys. That can change if you don't check yourself."

Fred's eyes grew wide. He released Jerry's arm and shoved his hands in his pockets. "Where do you think you are going, McNeal?"

"To pack."

"We had a deal. You said you would look into this."

"The deal was I would look into it my way with no outside interference. If all you want is a finger man, there are plenty of clowns out there that will gladly do your bidding. Get one of them because I won't help you turn the key on this guy unless I'm sure."

"What makes you so sure he's not our guy?"

Jerry sighed. "I didn't say he wasn't."

"Then what are you saying?"

"I'm saying stay out of this. You are too close and are letting your personal feelings cloud your judgment. If Nick Stringer is your guy, I will personally help you drag him into the courtroom." Jerry knew the rules. No body, no crime. But if he had even an inkling the guy was guilty, he had ways of getting a confession. If the dog couldn't worm it out of him, he'd call his uncle Marvin in on the session and make it a family affair. With Marvin's mind-reading abilities, he would have Nick singing like a canary in no time flat. Jerry hoped it wouldn't come to that as, thus far, neither Fred nor Barney knew just how talented his inner circle really was.

Fred smiled. "I thought you said you don't hang around to see the messy part."

Jerry shrugged. "I don't normally. But this case is different – there's a kid involved."

Fred's mouth twitched. "We are going to get the sonofa…"

Jerry cut him off. "If he's guilty."

Fred rocked back on his heels. "So, what's your plan?"

"My plan is to go have a chat with him."

Fred smiled. "You're going there now?"

Jerry nodded. "Yep."

"That's more like it. Let me grab my keys. I'll go with you."

Jerry looked at Gunter, half wishing to order the dog to bite the guy. Gunter was watching and took a step forward. Jerry held up his hand. "No!"

Fred took a step back. "What's your deal, McNeal?"

Jerry ran a hand over his head and blew out a long breath. "My brother died."

"Yeah, I read something about that."

Fred had done his homework before making contact. That the man knew about Joseph's death didn't surprise him. "I'm sure you did. What you didn't know is I was responsible."

Fred arched an eyebrow. Jerry shook off the accusation. "I didn't kill him. But I could have prevented it." Jerry held up his hands to ward off any questions. "The thing of it is, I know what it's like to feel like your hands are tied and you can't do what it is you do. I know you want this guy so bad, you are willing to sacrifice your career to do it. So bad that you've lain in bed figuring out ways to disappear the guy so that nobody would know it was you. But you didn't. Not because you don't have it in you – you didn't because there is a part of you that just isn't convinced he's the guy. You've had your shot at him. Now let me do my job. That's why I'm here, right?"

Fred relented. "Okay, McNeal. We'll do it your way."

Jerry clapped the guy on the shoulder. "I'll get you answers. It's what I do."

Fred nodded a pinched mouth nod. "I know. That's why I asked you to come."

Chapter Seven

It only took a few moments to make the short drive to the Lamphere Road address listed for Nick. Gunter followed Jerry to the door and waited by his side for the man to answer.

The door opened, and a purple-haired woman who looked to be in her mid-twenties narrowed her eyes at him. "Whatever you're selling, we ain't buying."

What was the wife's name? Jerry went over the report in his mind. *Beverly, yeah, that's it.* He held up his hands. "Mrs. Stringer, it's Beverly, right? I'm not a solicitor."

Beverly's eyes narrowed further. "You think you're going to get somewhere by knowing my name? The whole blasted town knows my name. Now, what do you want?"

"I'd like to speak with Nick." Jerry worked to make his request sound like that of an old friend.

She placed a hand on her hip and showed no sign of opening the door any further. "Nick's not home."

So much for an easy entry. Jerry nodded to Gunter. The dog stuck his head through the door, then pushed his way further before disappearing. If Nick was in there, the K-9 would flush him out. *Stay cool, McNeal. Give the dog time for a thorough search of the place.* "If Nick's home, I'd really like to have a few words with him."

The area around her lips turned white as she pinched them together. When she spoke, she did so through gritted teeth. "I already told you Nick's not home. You a cop? Cause if you are, I'm going to call our attorney and let him know you're harassing us again."

That Fred had been relentless in his pursuit didn't come as a surprise. Jerry shook his head. "I'm not a cop."

His denial didn't faze her. "You must be another one of those reporters, then? We already told you guys that we don't have nothing to say."

Though the town received a lot of visitors during tourist season, it was still a small town. Like most small towns, Jerry suspected they would be eager for news, especially if the news would make a good front-page story. Jerry shook his head. "No, ma'am, I'm not a reporter either."

Beverly blew out a disgusted sigh. "Then what do you want?"

The woman was cynical and had every right to be. A year of living under suspicion would make anyone so. *Stick to the truth, McNeal. The woman is smart and will see through any ruse.* "I just want to help."

She laughed a skeptical laugh. "Help put my husband behind bars is more like it."

Stay calm, McNeal. That she hasn't already slammed the door in your face is a promising sign. "If that's where he belongs, then yes."

Her eyes grew wide.

It was easy to see he'd caught her off guard. *Come on, McNeal, you can do this.* Jerry kept his voice nonjudgmental. "I told you I'm here to help, and it's the truth. I came here to see Nick. But I'm going to lay things out for you. Here's the way I see the situation. You love your husband."

She gave a slight nod.

Jerry continued before she could speak. "At first, you fully believed Nick when he told you he didn't have anything to do with the child's disappearance. But over the last year, the people in charge of the case have hounded both you and your husband, trying to get something they can use against him."

Beverly's mouth twitched.

Jerry could see he was getting to her and continued. "Nick has become exceedingly moody over the last few months. Your marriage is strained, and every now and then, when you stare at your husband, you wonder if maybe you're wrong. That just maybe he did do what everyone is claiming he did. Does that sound about right?"

"What are you, some kind of mind reader?" The

words came out in a whisper, and Jerry knew he'd read her correctly. Not that this particular reading had much to do with his gift; he'd watched enough *CSI* to know how things worked.

"Not a mind reader. I'm a psychic. I can help you if you let me." Jerry knew his words could have the opposite effect of what he'd intended, especially if the woman didn't believe in such things.

"How?"

Jerry was relieved by the tinge of hope he'd detected in her voice. "By getting to the truth."

"You mean by locking Nick away!"

Jerry sighed. He was losing her. "Only if Nick is guilty."

"It won't matter. Mr. Jefferies is convinced Nick is guilty. He's told me so on more than one occasion. I don't know what the man's problem is, but I can tell you this. It doesn't matter if Nick is guilty or not. Mr. Jefferies won't be satisfied until Nick is in prison."

Gunter appeared at Jerry's side. That the dog hadn't alerted him told him the woman was telling the truth about Nick not being at home.

Obviously, Fred had not been upfront with them. If he had, Beverly and Nick would already know of his connection to the case and thus understand why he was hounding them. It also showed that Fred had let his personal feelings get in the way. Something that didn't bode well for the prosecutor if Nick were, in fact, responsible for the girl's disappearance. Jerry smiled a disarming smile. "Mr. Jefferies is the one who sent me. He asked me to look into the disappearance."

"You're working for him? That means you'll lie for him as well. You come onto my porch trying to worm your way inside with all this psychic mumbo jumbo. Why on earth would I want to help you frame my husband?"

Jerry slid his foot into the opening just as Beverly moved to close the door. "No, ma'am, I won't. I give you my word that I am not in Jefferies' pocket. That is why he is not here with me. I told him the only way I would do this is if he didn't get in the way of my investigation. I don't owe him anything. I only want the truth."

She eased her grip on the door. "And Mr. Jefferies agreed to that?"

"Yes, ma'am. He wasn't pleased about not being able to come, but he agreed. You see, he wants to know the truth as much as we do. You do want to know, don't you?"

She was quick to nod her head.

"Good. Mr. Jefferies trusts me, and as such, he agreed to abide by my determination. If I say Nick is guilty, your husband will be arrested. If I find he wasn't involved, Mr. Jefferies promises to back off."

"You mean he will stop harassing us." She tucked her bottom lip under her top teeth, hanging on his answer.

He'd better. "Yes."

"What if you can't tell?"

Jerry looked her in the eye. "I will know. It is what I do. My grandmother called it a gift. Sometimes I'm not so sure. Either way, whatever it is works. All I have to do is talk with Nick, and I will be able to tell."

She wrung her hands as if trying to decide. "Nick is not going to be happy I'm talking to you. I'm not sure what to do."

"The only thing you have to do is tell me where to find your husband. I won't tell him how I found him." Jerry looked her in the eye. "I know the last year has been difficult for you and your family, but I promise you I'm on your side. I can't begin to imagine what it's been like for you, but wouldn't it be nice to find out now once and for all? If Nick was involved, then you will have some tough decisions to make. If he wasn't, you can stop being afraid of him."

Her head snapped up, and she heaved a sigh. Her lips trembled. When she next spoke, the hard edge she'd greeted him with was gone. "I believe him, at least I used to. Now, I just don't know. They make it all sound so convincing. We were planning on starting a family, but how can I even consider that with all that has transpired? Even our friends have turned their backs on us – most of them anyway.

Not that I blame them. Anytime Nick would have contact with anyone from our inner circle, then someone would show up and question them. Sometimes someone would show up at their work. I mean, it just isn't right, you know?"

Jerry wanted to tell her they needed a different attorney. Instead, he nodded his understanding. "Yes, ma'am. It's their way of keeping the pressure on, hoping someone in your inner circle will crack. But it is my job to know for sure."

"So, if you find out he's guilty, how does that work? Will he still have a trial, or will the judge just believe you because you know things?"

"I assure you we will follow the proper channels." *Careful making promises you might not be able to keep, McNeal. Fred finds out the guy is guilty, he may make sure the man never sees the inside of a courtroom.* Jerry ran his hand over the top of his head. "Let's not get ahead of ourselves. Tell me where I can find your husband, and we'll put an end to this one way or another."

Jerry could feel her internal struggle as she debated telling him. For a moment, he thought she would decline his request. Finally, she spoke. "He's at the marina. He helps with the boats. It's not much, but he doesn't get a lot of handyman work since the girl disappeared. It was worse right after she went missing. It got better for a bit, then people stopped calling. We found out someone was warning them off."

It didn't take a rocket scientist to know who that someone was. *Fred.* Jerry removed his foot from between the door and the jamb. "I promise we will get this resolved soon."

Beverly smiled a halfhearted smile. "One way or another, right?"

Jerry started to turn and hesitated. "I'd appreciate it if you don't tell Nick I'm heading his way."

She hung her head. "Don't worry. I'd rather not give him a reason to hate me."

Jerry managed a smile. "If he's innocent, he'll never have to run again."

She frowned. "I just realized I didn't get your name."

Way to go, McNeal, that's police academy kindergarten. Instead of getting into an argument with his inner conscience, Jerry reached a hand to the woman. "My grandmother is probably spinning in her grave at my lack of manners. Jerry McNeal. Nice to make your acquaintance."

She took his hand and held it in a grip much stronger than he'd expected. "Mr. McNeal, please don't make me regret opening that door."

Jerry wanted nothing more than to assure the woman everything was going to be all right. But the truth of the matter was he just didn't know. Something about what the woman had told him rang untrue. He wasn't sure if it was related to the case or just in what she'd said. The last thing he would do was give her any false hope, not after all she'd been through.

He started to pull his hand from hers, and she gripped it tighter. "Mr. McNeal, I lied. The truth of it is, I really don't know where my husband is. He could be at the marina, but he could be just about anywhere else as well." She let go of his hand, and her voice broke when next she spoke. "Please help make this right. I beg you not to take my husband away from me. We were so happy before all of this."

And there it was. Any reservations he'd had quickly dissipated. Still unable to make Beverly a promise he couldn't keep, Jerry simply nodded and left without another word.

Gunter beat him to the Durango and jumped inside without waiting for Jerry to open the door. Jerry didn't think the dog was eager to find Nick as much as to get away from the house. Whether Nick was guilty or not still remained to be determined, but one thing was clear – a veil of desperate energy hung over the dwelling, robbing the inhabitants of their happiness. If Jerry wasn't so confident in his abilities, he'd be in a heck of a position. As it was, he only needed a few moments alone with the guy to establish if the desperation was for the truth to be known so that the couple could move on with their lives, or for forgiveness for deeds that had long gone unpunished.

Chapter Eight

Jerry followed the navigator's directions, turning onto Cow Hill Road. The road changed names, and he continued on High Street, following it to West Main Street, also known as US-1, the main route he'd originally followed into town. He rolled to a stop at the corner of West Main and admired the Union Baptist Church sitting high on the upper corner. Surrounded by a stone retaining wall, the church was a formidable presence overlooking the main street of town.

Jerry was just getting ready to let off the brake when the church bells began to ring. Both beautiful and haunting, Jerry felt the hair on the back of his neck stand on end. So far, all of the victims of the Hash Mark Killer had told him they'd heard bells.

A horn sounded. Jerry rolled his neck and turned left onto West Main. *Easy, McNeal. It's not like you to get spooked.*

Jerry glanced at Gunter as if it were he who spoke. "I'm not spooked."

Gunter yawned.

The bells continued to ring their song as he drove

down the hill. He was so caught up in recalling what the victims had told him, he nearly missed seeing the sign for Mystic Pizza housed in a blue and grey building on the left side of the road within view of the church. That it had a Brew Pub next door was an added bonus.

Jerry felt himself starting to relax. He turned to Gunter once more. "Don't let me forget to get a picture of that for Max and her mom."

Gunter answered with a single woof and a wag of the tail.

Jerry laughed. "I'll take that as a yes."

As Jerry passed Pearl Street, he thought about leaving the Durango at the house and walking to the marina but decided against it, knowing Fred would be watching for him to return. Though traffic was heavy, it stopped only when a car would pull out from the curb, and vehicles would pause long enough for another to parallel park in its place.

A couple walked along the sidewalk, pulled by a caramel and white basset hound puppy whose ears nearly dragged on the ground. Gunter whined then stuck his head through the glass for a closer look. Jerry crossed over the drawbridge and made a right onto Cottrell Street. He saw an empty parking space just past the juice bar and whipped the Durango into the spot. Gunter pulled his head inside the moment Jerry turned off the engine. Tongue hanging from his mouth, his tail wagged, showing he was eager to explore.

That Jerry didn't feel a pull let him know Nick was not in the area, but as he didn't have anything else to do, he got out and started walking toward the marina. Gunter ran in front of him, nose to the ground, following an invisible path.

Jerry left the dog to his own devices as he followed the sidewalk to the water and continued walking toward the marina. He heard giggles and turned to see Gunter standing in the grass wagging his tail. Though Jerry couldn't see anyone, it was obvious from the dog's playful demeanor he wasn't alone. Not wishing to frighten the spirit, who'd elected to remain invisible, Jerry continued toward the marina. Every so often, he stopped and pretended to stare off into the inlet in hopes of getting a glimpse of Gunter's newfound playmate. At one point, he saw the misty outline of what could be construed as a small child, but that was the extent of anything remotely ghostly other than the dog.

The marina was busy, with most of the slips full. Jerry walked around the wooden docks looking for Nick even though he couldn't feel him there. Once finished, Jerry began walking back the way he'd come. Though he enjoyed the serene beauty of the small seaport village, the seagulls screeching their calls reminded him of Rita Wadsworth. A victim of the Hash Mark Killer, Rita had mentioned hearing the seagulls as the man was abducting her. Jerry rolled his neck, suddenly regretting having allowed himself to be lured off the case. His heart rate increased. *What am I doing here when they need me?*

Gunter yipped. Jerry turned to see the ghostly K-9 lowered into a playful bow as he continued to play with his unseen playmate.

An image of the little girl from the photo came to mind. *She needs me too. How am I going to help her if she doesn't allow me to get close to her?* Jerry took a deep breath and ran a hand over his head to help calm himself. *Give it time, McNeal. Just give it some time.*

Jerry returned to the house on Pearl Street, not in the least surprised to see Fred's car in the driveway. He turned off the engine, got out, and leaned against the driver's side door. He didn't have to wait long. Fred pushed open the back door, crossing the distance in long strides. Jerry knew what the man wanted and what his response would be.

Best get it over with, McNeal. Jerry listened to his inner voice, stopping Fred before the man had a chance to ask. "He wasn't home."

"What do you mean he wasn't home? Where was he?"

Jerry ran a hand over his head. "No clue."

Fred looked at his watch. "It took you two hours to drive five minutes and find out the guy wasn't home?"

Jerry leveled a look at the man. "Last I saw,

neither myself nor Nick Stringer requires a babysitter."

Fred's ears turned pink. "You're getting a bit defensive over a guy you say you've never met."

Gunter took exception to Fred's tone and moved between the two men.

That's because things are not adding up. Jerry kept that thought to himself as he looked at the house and then back to Fred. "Is there anyone in there waiting for you, or do you have time for a beer?"

The tension left Fred's shoulders. "I could go for a cold one."

Jerry thought about inviting the man up. After all, he purchased the beer currently chilling in his fridge. *Don't do it, McNeal. Take him someplace you can leave if things turn sour.* Jerry smiled. "I saw a Brew Pub. The building was impressive. Is the beer any good?"

Fred nodded. "Bank & Bridge Brewing, it's the old Bank building. I've been there a time or two."

"You want to drive or use our legs?" Though he himself would prefer to walk, Jerry wasn't sure Fred was up for the task, mainly because the man was wearing a suit and dress shoes.

Fred shrugged. "I could use a walk. It's only a few blocks away."

At the mention of the word "walk," Gunter forgot all about being in protection mode and spun in excited circles.

***

Inside the former bank building was bright white and cheerful. They ordered at the bar, Jerry opting to step out of his comfort zone of Bud and a burger, ordered a Mystic IPA and the PB&J Burger. Fred opted for a fish sandwich and the Manatee Porter. The sign over the bar stated the place was Marine-owned. Though Jerry didn't know the man, he felt pride in a fellow Devil Dog's success.

A table opened up in the corner. Fred hurried to secure it while Jerry let the lady behind the bar know where they'd be sitting. The place was busy and rather loud. Gunter plastered himself to Jerry's leg and stayed by his side as Jerry took a chair with his back to the wall where he could observe at a distance.

"You always do that," Fred noted when Jerry joined him.

Jerry couldn't recall actually doing anything. "Do what?"

"Sit with your back to the wall."

Jerry shrugged. "I guess it feels better."

"You mean safer?"

Another shrug. "I guess you can say that."

Fred chuckled. "You travel with a dog that no one can see, and you're afraid to sit with your back to the room."

Jerry took a sip of his beer. *Not bad.* He took another drink before sitting his glass down. "I've never been much for crowds."

Fred looked around the room. "Is that why you opted to sit outside at the hotdog joint in Salem?"

Nope, that was because I didn't trust that you didn't have the place bugged for sound. Jerry kept that thought to himself. He looked about the room, wondering. Then again, it was so noisy, he doubted a bug would do much good.

Fred interrupted his thoughts. "We can sit outside if you want."

Jerry mulled it over and shook his head. "No, I'm good."

The woman from the bar came over and set silver trays in front of them. She smiled at Jerry before hurrying back to her place behind the bar. Jerry turned the tray, inspecting the burger.

Fred plucked a fry from his own tray and pointed it at Jerry. "You going to eat it or sit there looking at it?"

"I haven't decided." Jerry smiled, took out his phone, and snapped a picture of it.

Fred raised an eyebrow. "Do you always take pictures of your food?"

Suddenly self-conscious, Jerry picked up his burger and took a bite. The unorthodox burger was sloppy but remarkably tasty. Still holding on to the burger, he lifted it for Fred to see. "Not bad, but I wouldn't recommend eating one while wearing a white shirt."

Fred nodded his agreement. “You going to eat something like that, it’s best to dive into it and eat it without setting it down.”

The man had a point, especially since the sandwich was now in danger of slipping from beneath its bun. Jerry started on the sloppy delight, eating in silence as Fred worked on his mess-free meal. When Jerry finished, he licked off a glob of peanut butter that had dribbled onto the outside of his pinky. He picked up a napkin and wiped his hands clean. “Man, a sandwich like that makes you feel alive.”

Gunter pressed against the side of his leg. Jerry felt instant regret at having made the remark, a feeling heavily compounded when Jerry looked down and saw the line of drool hanging from the K-9’s mouth. Jerry sighed and reached for his beer.

“Why so glum? You looked as happy as a two-year-old the whole time you were eating.”

“It’s Gunter.”

Fred scanned the area around the table. “The dog? What’s wrong with him?”

“He’s drooling,” Jerry replied glumly.

“Ghosts can do that?”

“They can pretty much do anything they want.” Jerry thought about telling him about his grandmother making him a cup of tea for his headache but decided against it. It was enough the man believed in the dog and all the other bizarre things he'd presented him with.

Fred leaned back, looked under the table, and casually dropped a french fry on the ground, then peered at the fry as if expecting it to disappear. The action reminded him of his father, who'd done the same thing. A frown tugged at the man's lips when the fry remained untouched. "Doesn't he eat?"

"I've seen him gnaw on a bone, but it is one he brought with him from the other side." Jerry stopped short of mentioning that the bones were always bloody.

Fred sat back in his chair. "Maybe he just doesn't like fries."

"I tried him on a hot dog once. It seemed as if he wanted it but didn't actually try it."

Fred smiled. "I guess there are advantages of having a dog you don't have to feed."

Jerry nodded his agreement. That was the best thing about his newfound friend – the dog was on autopilot. A waitress stopped by. Jerry ordered them both another round of beers.

As soon as she was out of earshot, Fred lowered his voice. "So what's on your mind, McNeal? You've had a chip on your shoulder all evening."

The man was right, there were several things not setting well at the moment. Jerry ran a finger over the rim of his glass, debating where to start, and decided just to lay it on the line. "I don't like being played."

Fred's face remained impassive. "I'm not reading you."

Jerry leaned forward in his chair. "How about we cut through the crap."

Fred's energy changed.

Gunter pushed to his feet and moved around the table.

Jerry knew the dog had felt the shift and moved to keep a closer eye on the man.

"Just tell me the truth. We both know that's not your sister's house. You're trying so hard to have me come work wherever the heck it is you work, and you're still playing games. Not to mention the fact you have crossed so many lines that if Nick is guilty, the defense will probably be able to declare a mistrial before the thing even starts." Jerry sat back in his chair. "Maybe that's what you want… to get all eyes off the man so you can take care of him yourself."

Fred drained his glass before answering. "Rest assured, if I wanted to take the man out, I would have already done so."

"But you couldn't because you're not a hundred percent sure the man is responsible. You thought by needling Nick and his wife and alienating them from their friends, they would admit to it. Only they stuck to their story, and that is why you wanted me here. You need me to find out once and for all."

Fred nodded and backed out of the way as the

waitress set two beers in front of them. His energy calmer, Gunter returned to his place at Jerry's side.

Fred took a sip and lowered his glass. "You're right about that not being my sister's house. It's mine and the wife's house. My sister has never lived here, and I wish she and her family had never visited. She and Angie came for an extended visit last year. My sister went out on a whale-watching tour out of Rhode Island the day Angie went missing. Tina was going to take Angie along, but the weather report said it might rain, and I insisted she leave the kid with me. I figured it would be safer. Anyway, we were a couple of miles from here visiting a friend. It had been raining for days, but that morning, it was mostly sprinkles. The kid wanted to go out and play, so I didn't see the harm. When the rain started again, I called for her to come inside. She never did."

Jerry watched as Fred picked up his glass and downed the brew in one smooth motion. Fred lowered the glass and wiped his lips with his thumb. "I've babysat mobsters so hot, they shouldn't have made it into the courtroom alive, and I couldn't keep tabs on a four-year-old kid."

Jerry understood the man's motivation. And on a personal level, he also understood the man's pain. He thought of his brother Joseph as he lifted his glass and drank to their kinship with the guilt of letting down those closest to you.

Chapter Nine

Jerry sat on a bench staring into the mist, hoping to see the little girl. The mist split into four, and suddenly, the known victims of the Hash Mark Killer were standing in front of him. Patti O'Conner peered at him with tear-brimmed eyes. Ashley Fabel glared at him with crossed arms. Rosie Freeman, who'd been cheerful the last time he'd seen her spirit, now glowered in his direction, the look sending chills up and down his spine. Rita Wadsworth wagged her finger at him. The intensity of their combined disdain had him taking a step back.

Jerry looked for Gunter. The dog was nowhere to be seen. *Gunter, I need you!* Several seconds went by, and still, the dog failed to appear.

Rita laughed a haunting laugh. "What's the matter, Jerry? Scared?"

Actually, yes. Better not tell them that. "No."

Instantly, Rita was directly in front of him, leaning over him. "You'd better be afraid. You don't think you can break your promise to us and get away with it, do you?"

Jerry leaned back in the chair to get away from the spirit whose face was only inches from his. "What promise? I didn't break any promise."

She grabbed his jaw, her slender fingers holding it so he couldn't look away. He watched as finger-length bruises appeared on her neck, then one after one, others appeared, showing the horrors that preceded her death. Rita kept a death grip on his jaw as she turned his head to see each of the other women, who now each showed the atrocities they'd suffered at the hands of their killer. "You promised to find the man who did this to us."

Jerry tried to pull away, but her grip was too strong. *Where is Gunter?* The dog was supposed to protect him.

Rita laughed and pushed his head back so far, he nearly tipped backwards in his chair. She released him on another laugh, the sound just as wicked as the one before. "He's gone."

Gunter's gone? That can't be.

"Don't be a fool. He ran off with the child you came here to find."

Jerry realized she'd read his mind. "Get out of my head."

"Too late. You didn't block us, and now we are all in here learning all of your secrets. Feasting on your fears." Rita moved forward. Ashley and Rosie moved up beside her, dragging a reluctant Patti along with them.

Patti's tears fell against his cheek. She wiped them away with her hand. He tried to move away, but she kept brushing his cheek. A tear fell into Jerry's ear, and she quickly wiped it away. Jerry brought his hand up, felt something furry, and knew Gunter had returned.

Jerry opened his eyes and saw the massive shepherd hovering over him. His head lowered as he snaked his tongue across Jerry's face.

Only a dream. The relief was instant. Jerry dug his hands into the K-9's fur, grateful the dog had not abandoned him. Gunter lapped at Jerry's ear several more times before, feeling calmer, Jerry finally pushed the K-9's head away. Jerry looked at the clock on the nightstand. *Just after five. That's it for me.* He rose, went to the dresser, and pulled out his running clothes. The moment he reached for his tennis shoes, Gunter raced to the door spinning in excited circles.

Though Gunter raced down the stairs, Jerry took his time. He walked to the Durango and lifted his foot on the tire to stretch out the muscles in his leg before repeating the process with the other leg.

Gunter sneezed.

Jerry remembered reading that dogs sometimes sneezed when they were enjoying themselves. That Gunter now stood in the driveway wagging his tail reiterated this. Feeling more like himself, Jerry managed a smile. It had been way too long since they'd run together. He finished stretching and started toward Main Street.

The town was practically empty, traffic nearly nonexistent, making it easy to run without worry. With no destination in mind, Jerry just ran. After several moments, Gunter pulled ahead of him and appeared to be on a mission. Jerry followed, happy to let the K-9 determine which way they'd go. They made a left onto Holmes, another on Greenmanville. They passed the Mystic Seaport Museum, which took up both the left and right side of the road, and kept running. The next block hosted white houses with white fencing cordoning off the front yard. Some of the houses had what appeared to be placards. The next group of houses proved to be more stately, with ornate wrought-iron fencing that lined the sidewalk in front of them. From the looks of the fencing, Jerry guessed it to have been put in at the same time the houses were built.

As they continued down the street, he saw a sign stating it to be the north entrance to the museum. Jerry realized all the houses they'd just run past were all part of an elaborate historical display.

The houses thinned out and, in time, were replaced with a water view. They ran past a tiny ice cream shop. Jerry made a mental note to stop in later that day. A thigh-high stone fence proved host to a cemetery that paralleled the water and seemed to go on for quite some time. Jerry followed as Gunter made a right on Coogan Road and continued up the hill without a backward glance. A red barn-style building with eye-catching letters that read STEAK LOFT caught his eye. Jerry's stomach rumbled. As he passed the McDonald's, Jerry was feeling a bit winded. *Come on, McNeal, don't be a wuss.* Jerry dug deep and lengthened his stride, watching as Gunter rounded the bend ahead of him.

Jerry noted a Holiday Inn on the right and what looked to be a sizable cluster of shops to the left. Once again, he made a mental note to come back and check out the area. Provided they would eventually stop running. The landscape evened out. Jerry lucked out to keep going through the traffic light that turned green just as he reached it.

Gunter crossed the road a short distance later and headed into the parking lot. Jerry looked for cars and followed to see the dog had led him to the Mystic Seaport Aquarium. The parking lot was empty, aside from a handful of cars parked at the far end of the lot. Gunter stopped near the front of the building. For the first time, he looked as if to see if Jerry had followed.

Jerry slowed and wiped the sweat from his brow. As he worked to control his breathing, he looked at the building that loomed in front of him, then back at the dog that didn't even have the courtesy to hang his tongue out of his mouth.

"Dude, the least you could do is pretend to look

winded."

Gunter opened his mouth, rolled out his tongue, and started panting.

Jerry laughed. "Much better. Now, why are we here?"

Gunter walked toward the entrance, stopped, and turned to see if Jerry was following.

Jerry stood his ground. "You do know the place is closed, right?"

Gunter barked and walked to the entrance. He looked through the gate and wagged his tail.

"What's gotten into you, dog?" Jerry walked to where Gunter was standing and peered through the opening. He scanned the area that was reserved for paying guests. As his gaze moved to the right, he froze. There, next to a concrete enclosure, was a small child. Her brown hair pulled into pigtails, she wore a pink and green shorts outfit. The child stood on her tippytoes in lime-green crocs, looking at whatever was on the other side of the enclosure. Jerry heard a squeak. The child's spirit imitated the sound.

Gunter cocked his head to the side, then moved through the locked gates with ease. When he reached her, he jumped up, placing his paws on the top of the enclosure and looked over the side. The child giggled, Gunter wagged his tail, and Jerry felt totally left out, which was precisely where he was. Outside. *So much for superpowers.*

"Angie?"

The spirit whipped her head around, staring at him for several seconds. "I'm not Angie." She pushed from the enclosure and disappeared through the closed door of the building. Gunter followed without a backward glance.

Why the child denied her name, he wasn't sure. It was her. He was certain of it, as she matched the child in the picture. Not for the first time, Jerry struggled with his gift. Some gift, as he would now have to break the news to Fred and the child's parents. While the family already knew it, until it was made official, there would always be that tiny sliver of hope. A hope he would dash when he told them Angie was truly gone.

Gone from this world at least. Just like Gunter, the child was very much a part of something he would never truly understand. At least not in this lifetime.

Jerry checked the time and saw the aquarium was not scheduled to open for several hours. He turned and started walking the way he'd just come. He looked over his shoulder several times to see if Gunter was following. He wasn't. Jerry was torn. While he didn't blame the dog for staying with the girl, a part of him worried that the nightmare had been a premonition.

He looked over his shoulder once more and sighed. *I don't want another dog.*

Jerry started into a slow jog. After a few moments, he began to run. He thought about Angie and how happy the child's spirit seemed. Then an image of Fred came to mind. The man's agony of losing his niece heightened by the guilt of feeling responsible for her demise. How the child had perished, Jerry still didn't know. Nor was he sure how to break the news to the family. As his mind raced, his stride lengthened until he wondered if he was running toward his destination or away from things he couldn't control. In the end, he thought it might be a little of both.

As he turned onto Main Street, Jerry saw the drawbridge rising and slowed his pace. Checking his cell phone, he saw it was 7:40. He was near the building shaped like a lighthouse when he heard sirens shrieking behind him. A horn blared in the opposite direction, and the drawbridge started back down, solving his burning question from the previous day of what emergency personnel would do if the bridge were up when they got a call.

Jerry looked at the tall-masted sailboat currently heading toward the bridge. *It's a good thing it wasn't closer when the bridge changed its course.* Three firetrucks and a police vehicle crossed the bridge before the light changed, and the bridge once again started to rise. Jerry wasn't in any hurry and stayed back, admiring the mechanics of the bridge. He took a few photos of the bridge in action, making sure to include the massive concrete counterweights that helped with the maneuver.

Jerry stood next to the rail, stretching out his calf muscles and watching boats of all shapes and sizes make their way out of the river inlet toward their daily adventure. The boats made him think of the marina, which in turn made him think of Nick.

Jerry pushed off the rail and made his way to the marina hoping to find the man. This side of the bridge was no less active than the other, with water goers readying their crafts for open waters. Jerry walked up and down the wooden docks looking for anyone who might match Nick's description. He hadn't pinged on the guy but thought that maybe it was because the man was innocent of wrongdoing. *It's the only thing that makes sense.*

Jerry's stomach rumbled. He pulled out his phone and searched for a doughnut shop. He found a bake shop on Water Street. Finding Water Street was just up from Pearl, he started in that direction. As he rounded the corner, he saw Gunter standing in front of the building at the end of the street. The dog looked up when Jerry approached and wagged his tail.

The fact that the K-9 appeared happy to see him warmed his heart. "What are you doing, boy?"

Gunter stuck his head through the glass as his tail continued to wag.

Even before he looked in the window, Jerry

knew Angie was inside, as the hair on the back of his neck was prickling. Jerry cupped his hands over his eyes and peered through the glass. He smiled. Angie was sitting on the floor surrounded by a slew of mermaid dolls and stuffed animals. Oblivious to anything else, she was drinking pretend tea from plastic cups and jabbering to her newfound friends.

Jerry knocked on the window. Angie looked up, and Jerry waved. She frowned and turned her back to him but didn't disappear. Jerry wished for nothing more than to be able to snap a photo with his cell phone to show her family. Hoping for a miracle, Jerry did just that. He turned the phone to look at the photo, which showed nothing but clothing hanging on racks within the small space. *Why am I seeing toys?*

Jerry used his phone to Google toy stores at the same address and smiled at discovering that, until recently, the store was, in fact, a toy store.

Jerry started to knock on the window and changed his mind. She knew he could see her, and yet the knowledge hadn't frightened her away.

They were making progress. It was but a small victory, but a victory all the same.

Chapter Ten

Still reeking from his morning run, Jerry ordered a coffee and pecan sticky bun to go. He took his breakfast and sat at one of the outside tables enjoying the gooey delight. Now that he wasn't exerting himself, the morning air felt crisp. He welcomed the warmth of the sun beaming across his shoulders.

Something brushed his leg, and a tingle traveled along his neck. *Gunter.*

A second later, the dog materialized. Gunter sniffed at the table, licked his lips, then stretched into a downward dog before lowering to the ground. Jerry had positioned himself facing the street and now sat in compatible silence, watching as the town began to wake.

An elderly man wearing blue jeans and a flannel shirt walked through the opening of the patio with a faded coffee cup in his hand. His eyes searched each table before coming to rest on Jerry, who acknowledged the fellow with a nod. The man started forward, and Jerry thought he would join him at the table. Instead, the man sat next to a woman with silver hair having coffee at a nearby table. The moment he took his seat, the woman rubbed her shoulders. The man started chatting, and the woman, caught up in her own thoughts, ignored his words. The man palmed his cup and frowned. A frown that etched deeper when the woman finished her drink and left the patio without a word.

The man scowled as he pushed from his chair and joined Jerry at his table. He slammed a leathered fist on the table. "What are we going to do about her?"

Jerry looked at the man over the brim of his cup. "We?"

"Yes, we. I'm demanding that you talk to her. We have things that need fixing."

Jerry looked up and saw the women at the next table looking at him out of the corner of her eye and wished he'd remembered the Bluetooth Fred had given him. He picked up his phone, pretended to make a call, and placed it to his ear. "That's not the way it works. The woman knows I'm here. If she wants to speak to me, she will."

Hoping to get his point across, the man slammed his cup down on the table.

Gunter rose to his feet. Jerry held out a hand to settle the dog. The man eyed the K-9 but made no effort to lower his voice. "Well, if that don't beat all. I thought you were supposed to help us."

Jerry rolled his neck. *How is this my life?* "I'm

not a marriage counselor."

"I don't need a marriage counselor. I need you to talk to my wife."

Jerry raised a hand to settle the man. "Have you asked her what the problem is?"

"I already know the problem." The man grumbled. "I want to travel, and she wants to hang around the house and watch after the kids."

"If that's what she wants, then that's her prerogative."

"She's my wife."

Was. Obviously, the man hadn't heard the 'til death do us part of the marriage vows. Jerry ran a hand over his head. "What's your name?"

"Ralf. Ralf Emmerson. My wife's name is Emily."

No guts, no glory Marine. Jerry looked Ralf in the eye. "You know you're dead, right?"

The man held his gaze. "What do you mean I'm dead?"

Emily appeared. Standing over the man, she wagged a finger at Jerry. "Thank you! I've been trying to tell him that for years."

"Hogwash. When did you tell me that?"

"Right after you died. I told you that you were free to leave."

Ralf screwed up his face. "Well, dang, woman. I didn't know that meant I was dead. I thought you were asking for a divorce!"

Emily placed her hands on her hips. “We don’t need no divorce. That contract expired when you did.”

Ralf vanished.

Though she didn’t move her head, Emily’s gaze darted from side to side. “Is he gone?”

You’d probably know better than me. Jerry nodded. “Appears to be.”

She lowered her hands from where they rested on her hips. “Huh.”

Jerry couldn’t tell if that *huh* was good or bad. He started to ask when she too disappeared without another word. Jerry sat his cellphone on the table and looked at Gunter. “I guess I’ll never know.”

Gunter answered with a woof.

Jerry took a drink of his coffee. *Cold.* He set it aside and picked up his fork. The pastry was too good to toss no matter what the temperature. As he chewed, he thought about the ghostly couple – further wondering about their lives when living. Had they gotten along, or had they spent their lives bickering? He thought that to be the case – why else would Ralf have thought Emily had asked for a divorce?

He thought about his parents, who for all practical purposes seemed to get along well – would they choose to spend eternity together as well? His mind drifted further to the spirits he’d just met in Salem. For the most part, all seemed content to work together in the afterlife. He chuckled – as long as all spirits stayed in their own swim lane.

He sighed. It seemed the more he knew, the more questions he had. Questions he'd probably never have answers to until the time came that he no longer cared.

"You worry too much."

Jerry looked to see his granny sitting across the table from him. Gunter sprang to his feet, the bottom half of his body wiggling back and forth as he went to greet the ghostly spirit of Jerry's earthly grandmother.

The outside patio was quickly filling. Jerry picked up the phone, held it to his ear, and watched the woman frown. "I'm not ignoring you. The phone is to keep me from getting arrested for public crazy."

She raised an eyebrow. "Is that a thing now?"

Jerry blew out a sigh. "It is in my world." He smiled. "Is this a social visit or a life lesson?"

Granny was fawning over the dog. She paused in her petting. "I got the impression you needed me."

Another sigh. "I have so many questions, I don't even know where to begin."

Granny gave Gunter one last pat, clicking her tongue when the dog lifted his paw to her thigh, vying for more attention. Gunter returned to his spot beside Jerry, his ears on high alert for any sign the woman might change her mind. Granny leaned over his cup, sniffed the contents, and sat down again.

"Black. I never developed a taste for it that way. I always had to have a little sugar in it."

Jerry laughed, recalling the mounded spoons of sugar his grandmother used to scoop into her cup. "I think your idea of a little sugar is different from everyone else's."

She shrugged. "I was stingy in lots of ways. Being selfish with my sugar wasn't one of them."

"I don't recall a stingy bone in your body, at least not while you were alive."

She smiled and pressed an aged spotted hand over his. "What would be the fun of telling you all I know?"

"You didn't hesitate to share your knowledge when you were alive," he reminded her.

"That was different. The stakes are higher now."

What's that supposed to mean?

Granny winked and nodded toward the phone still plastered to his ear. "If you're going to pretend to use that thing, you might as well use your words, Jerry."

He smiled, realizing she'd heard what he'd been thinking. "It's this case I'm working on. I know the child is dead. I just don't know who did it. I don't know how to get her to trust me, and I am not sure how to tell Fred she's gone, much less what I'm supposed to say to her parents to ease their pain."

"You'll figure it out. You always do."

"I need to find this Nick guy, but my radar isn't

helping. He could be sitting at the table next to us, and I wouldn't know it. What does that mean?"

"What do you think it means?"

"That he's innocent?"

"People always have to have someone to blame."

"Does that mean I'm right?"

"It means just what I said. It is a burden of the living. The mom blames herself. Your friend blames himself, and everyone blames the man they believe responsible. If not for the blame, they might have to think it for what it really is."

"I'm tired of all the riddles. This isn't a puzzle; it is real life!" Jerry ran his hand over his head and eased his tone. "Why can't you just tell me what I need to know?"

"Because if I gave you all the answers, you wouldn't learn anything." She raised a hand, showing she wasn't done. "Life is a lesson, Jerry."

This was no other world revelation. His grandmother had used those words often when she was alive. He looked her in the eye. "And you believe that even now?"

"It is not what I believe. It is what I know. You learn something with each decision you make. Just like when you were little and touched the stove. You learned it was hot and never touched it again. It is the same now. Only it is up to you to decide if you are going to keep making the same mistake or learn from it."

He squeezed the phone a little tighter, not wishing to take his frustration out on the woman he still held so dear. "I have to tell Fred and the family that Angie is never coming back. What lesson is that supposed to teach me?"

"Angel."

"What?"

"She doesn't want to be called Angie anymore. She wants to be called Angel."

Jerry eased his grip on the phone. "Is that what she meant when she said her name wasn't Angie?"

The old woman smiled.

Jerry sat back in his chair. "What happened to not helping me?"

Granny beamed her delight. "There's a difference between presenting you with the holy grail of unearthly knowledge and giving you a little nudge in the right direction."

I don't like her spirit being alone. Jerry was about to voice the concern aloud when his grandmother spoke.

"She isn't alone."

"I haven't seen her with anyone else."

His grandmother was quiet for a bit as if deciding what to say. "She isn't a child anymore. Her spirit doesn't need to be looked over any more than an old lady who was once too old to remember where she'd left her reading glasses. She calls herself Angel because that is what she is. It is her job to watch over those who once watched over her. Now, you must convince those who mourn for her."

Jerry ran his hand over his head. "And just how am I supposed to do that?"

"You'll find a way, Jerry. You always do."

She started to fade. Jerry stopped her. "Wait, just answer one more question."

She appeared in full form. "If I can."

"When I was in Salem, a spirit told me they – he and others around him – had jobs. You haven't mentioned a job, but he was pretty sure of himself."

The lines around her eyes crinkled. "I was expecting you to ask the secrets of the universe."

He matched her smile. "I would but didn't think you'd tell me. So do you have a job?"

"I do."

His mind filled with a list of jobs she'd be qualified for. He stopped when she reached across the table and pulled the phone away from his ear, and sat it on the table in front of him. She placed a hand on his cheek. "My job is to watch over you."

Gunter barked a grumbling bark.

"And you too, Gunter." Though she disappeared, her chuckles lingered.

Several of those sitting near looked about as if they too had heard the woman's laughter carried in the wind. Slowly, they returned to their tasks when nothing seemed out of place.

Chapter Eleven

Gunter stayed at Jerry's side as he followed a couple out of the courtyard. Holding hands and talking about their plans for the day, they stepped into the crosswalk and continued across the street without looking. Even though he hadn't gotten a hit on his psychic radar, Jerry was relieved when traffic stopped, allowing the couple safe passage. He waved his thanks to the lead car, then followed the couple across the street. Pedestrians might have the right of way, but with the number of out-of-state plates he'd seen since being in town, there had to be some that weren't aware of the law. With that in mind, he had no intention of stepping off any curb without checking to ensure the driver had gotten the memo.

Unfazed by his concern, the couple took a left, heading up the hill, while he and several others that had crossed with him took a right and headed down toward the shops.

Gunter's energy changed.

Jerry heard the familiar whine of a Mini Cooper as the dog's head whipped around. Sure enough, it was the woman they'd seen during their initial drive into town. The top was still down on the Mini, and the white boxer took up the entire passenger seat. It was only as they passed that Jerry realized the dog was a spirit. The Mini slid into a parking space that paralleled the street, and Jerry hurried to reach the car as the woman got out.

An attractive woman, she wore a bright yellow sundress with a matching scarf. The headdress must only have been to keep her hair from flying into her face while driving as she pulled it from her head before stepping out of the car. She was surprisingly tall, her dress enticingly short, and as she exited, she began to reach for something. The dog stood in the seat, wagging the stump tail. She drew her hand back and shut the door without acknowledging the dog and slammed the door. She saw Jerry staring and looked him up and down. "I hope you're not planning to ask me to go running with you."

"No, ma'am, just checking out your car." Actually, he wanted to ask about the dog but wasn't sure how to broach the subject.

"My car is over there," she replied tersely.

Jerry realized he'd been staring at her legs. "Yes, ma'am. I was just appreciating how much leg room the thing has. Pretty nice passenger seat as well."

She leaned against the side of the car and crossed her slender legs. "I'm not sure if you are after me or my car."

Neither. At least he hadn't thought so until she called him on it. An image of Holly came to mind, and he brushed it aside. *Think of something clever, McNeal.* "I guess I hoped it would be a package deal." Jerry wanted to roll his eyes at the comment, but she beat him to it.

She smiled a genuine smile. "You're not very good at this, are you?"

He wasn't sure what "this" was but knew he was not making a good first impression. "Apparently not."

"It is for the best. I'm not ready to let anyone use that seat just yet."

Jerry craned his neck toward the car, and the boxer's backside wiggled. "What's wrong with the seat?"

"Nothing, other than the fact it's empty. It was Marley's seat. She was my boxer." The loss must have been recent, as the woman was now close to tears. Marley felt the woman's sorrow and stood in the seat whining.

Gunter, oblivious to Marley's concern, had his paws on the side of the passenger side door, his head leaning inside the car, sniffing the dog's nether region.

"Stop that!" Though Jerry directed the comment toward Gunter, he kept his eyes trained on the woman who now looked ready to scream for help.

Jerry held up his hands. "I'm sorry, I didn't mean

to yell at you. I just can't stand to see a woman cry."

"So you thought yelling at me would prevent it."

Way to go, McNeal. She thinks you're a kook. You might as well tell her what's on your mind. "Your dog is in the car. She is snow white and wearing a red collar that nearly matches the car."

She narrowed her eyes. "Great, and here I just thought you were weird. Not a class A jerk. That doesn't prove anything. You could've gotten that from my Facebook page."

Ouch. Jerry smiled a weak smile. "Okay, I guess I deserved that. But I assure you, I have not been stalking your Facebook page."

"So, what, do you get some kind of perverted pleasure from preying on people who are grieving?"

The fact that she hadn't stormed off told him she either wanted to believe him or was waiting for the perfect opportunity to kick him in a place that would bring her the most pleasure and him the most discomfort. Jerry hoped for the least painful solution for all parties.

"Listen, I know it sounds crazy, but I'm telling you, your dog is right there." He pointed to the dog, who now sat staring at him with her head cocked to the side.

Her eyes narrowed further. "Nice try, jerk. I look over there, and you grab my purse and run. I hate to break it to you, but I wasn't born yesterday."

Jerry looked at Gunter, who'd tired of his up

close and personal game and was now standing next to him, ears tilted as if to say, *You're on your own with this one, Marine.*

Jerry pulled himself taller and squared his shoulders. "I'm not a con man. I'm a cop. Or, at least I used to be. I'm also a guy who can see and speak with spirits of those who've passed. And yes, that includes dogs."

If he were a con artist, he would now have a golden opportunity to do whatever it was he had in mind as the woman had let down all her defenses and was currently holding her stomach as her laughter came out in snorts.

Jerry looked at Gunter, willing the dog to hear his thoughts. *I thought we were partners. Partners work together, remember? Do something. Jump up on her, bump into her, anything to get her to stop laughing.*

Gunter moved up beside the woman, leaning into her leg.

It worked. The woman gulped and looked down. Seeing nothing, she stared at Jerry with her mouth agape. "How'd you do that?"

Jerry shook his head. "I didn't do anything. Marley did."

Both dogs eyed him accusingly. Jerry sighed. *Ease up, you two. She barely believes me as it is. No way I'm telling her there's two of you.*

Gunter yawned but made no move to leave.

Marley barked, and Gunter placed a paw on the woman's foot.

Her eyes flew open as she stared at the ground by her feet. "She's stepping on my foot! She used to do it all the time, and I'd fuss at her. This morning, I started crying and said I wished she was still here and could step on my foot just one more time. Why is she still here? I thought there was some kind of rainbow bridge or something."

This was the part of the job Jerry didn't like. The part filled with questions to which he had no answers. "The truth of the thing is, I don't know what is out there. Or why some spirits allow themselves to be seen and others don't."

"Well, why not? If you can talk to them, you should have all the answers."

One would think so. Jerry shrugged. "I only know what I know and what I know is Marley is still with you. I've seen her a couple of times."

"You have?"

"Yes. Both times, she was sitting in the passenger seat having the time of her life." Jerry realized what he'd said. "She was enjoying herself."

"Does she…" The woman looked down and lowered her voice. "Does she look healthy?"

Jerry started to tell her the dog looked full of life and stopped. "Yes."

Gunter took this opportunity to move away from the woman.

"Where'd she go?"

"She's sitting in the car."

"What do I do now?"

"There's nothing to do. You go on with your life. You don't have to feed her or take her out." He smiled. You can talk to her but be careful. People will probably think you've lost your mind."

A blush crept over her face. "I'm sorry I didn't believe you. Too bad you're not still a cop. You could have just flashed a badge."

Jerry cocked an eyebrow. "Are you going to stand there and tell me you would have believed me any more if I had a badge?"

She giggled. "No. I suppose not. I wouldn't have believed you if I hadn't felt her myself. She must be doing okay. She felt a lot heavier than I remember."

Jerry turned so she couldn't see his face. He hated deceiving the woman, but if he hadn't used Gunter as a stand-in, she never would have believed him.

Her cell phone chimed. She looked at it and sighed. "I have to go."

Jerry nodded his understanding. *Don't be a sap, McNeal. Ask the woman out.* He was about to follow his conscience, when she clapped the side of her leg with her hand. Marley jumped out, her nub wagging from side to side.

The woman looked to him for confirmation. "Did it work?"

"It did. She's standing right next to you."

The woman beamed her delight. "I can't wait to tell my boyfriend. He's going to be shocked."

Of course she has a boyfriend. Jerry grabbed the back of his neck with his hand. "I'm sure he will."

She started to walk away and hesitated. "I didn't get your name."

"Jerry. Jerry McNeal." *King of missed opportunities.*

"Cool. My name's Crissy Layne. Do you have a Facebook page, Jerry? Maybe you can give my boyfriend and me a reading?"

Jerry shook his head. "I'm not that kind of psychic."

"Bummer. Thanks again. Maybe I'll see you around sometime."

As Jerry watched her walk down the street jabbering away to the dog only she could see, he suddenly wondered if he'd made a mistake in letting her know of her ghostly companion. He looked at Gunter. "The next time I decide to do a good deed, bite me."

Gunter lifted his lips to show his teeth.

Jerry laughed and patted the K-9 on the head. "Forget I asked."

***

Jerry was just stepping out of the shower when his cell rang. He checked the number. *Fred.* He debated letting it go to voice mail but knew the guy would take that as a reason to pound on the door. He wrapped the towel around him and answered the call. “Yeah?”

“I thought you were here to do a job, not take a vacation,” Fred snapped.

“If I was on vacation, I’d be enjoying myself,” Jerry replied, matching his tone.

“Well, you sure as heck aren’t doing what you came here to do.”

“That’s a matter of opinion.”

Fred’s tone softened. “Does that mean you have something?”

Yes, but nothing I care to share. Jerry opted to take the safe route. “I’m still working on it.”

“So you do have something?”

Jerry debated telling him about the couple and the dog but doubted either would improve the man’s sour mood. “When I have something solid, I’ll let you know.”

“How’s this for solid? I just got a call from Stringer’s wife. She told me she didn’t have a contact number for you. Didn’t you leave her a card?”

“I don’t have cards. What did she want?”

“She wanted me to tell you Nick is home. I don’t know what you said to the woman, but it worked. She’s been tight-lipped since this all went down.”

“I told her I could get to the truth.”

“Yeah, well, you’d best get to it. She said he’s

getting ready to mow the grass, so he'll be there for a bit."

"I'll head over as soon as I get dressed."

"Dressed? It's nearly eleven. I thought you were an early riser."

Jerry clicked off the phone without responding and tossed the phone on the bed next to the dog. As it landed, he heard a chime. Gunter raised his head as if to investigate.

"Don't worry, it's just Fred. He probably wants to yell at me some more. Maybe he's the one who needs to get bit. I'm kidding, by the way." As Jerry dressed, he continued his conversation with the dog. "Can you believe the morning we've had? We've played marriage counselor and reunited a woman and her dog."

Gunter yawned a grumbling yawn.

"I know you found the girl. I was getting to that." At least he thought he was. It didn't escape his notice that he seemed to be doing everything except what it was he should be doing.

Gunter crouched on the bed, watching Jerry's every move with an accusing gaze.

Jerry rolled his neck. "Don't look at me like that. I'll tell him just as soon as I have something to tell."

Gunter nosed the cell phone closer to the side of the bed.

Jerry snatched it from the covers. "No, I'm not going to call him. Things like that don't get told over the phone."

Gunter groaned and laid his head on his paws, watching Jerry's every move.

Jerry looked at the phone. *Huh.* The notification hadn't been from Fred after all. He pulled up the message from Max. > "I drew a picture of my mom. My teacher said it was pretty good. What do you think?"

Jerry clicked on the file and brought up the photo. *Wow.* Not only was the picture an incredible likeness, but Jerry wondered why he hadn't realized how attractive April was. *Why didn't I notice? Because you were too busy pining over someone else. Someone who has yet to give you the time of day. Shake it off, McNeal.* Jerry hit reply. *Tread carefully, McNeal. You don't want to give the kid the wrong idea.* > "Great job, Max. It's a beautiful photo of your mother."

The phone lit up with a new text from Max. > "Thanks. The teacher says I have a natural talent."

Jerry recalled the photo she'd drawn of him and Gunter. He hit reply. > "Your teacher is right. You may have found your calling. You really have a knack for it." He hit send and looked at the picture she'd sent once more. April wasn't a raving beauty, but pretty all the same. There was something about the way Max had captured the hope in her mother's eyes. *I guess it's easy to have hope when you no longer have to worry about having a roof over your head or if your daughter, who claims to see ghosts, needs therapy.* Jerry was pulled from his musings when his phone lit up.

Max> "Are you alright, Jerry? You seem confused."

Jerry worked to clear his mind. > "I'm good. It's just this case I'm working on. It's hard when there are kids involved. I've got to go for now. We'll talk later."

Gunter rolled onto his side with a groan.

Jerry shook his finger accusingly. "Stay out of this. I wasn't talking about Max."

Gunter closed his eyes, his lips curling into a K-9 grin.

Chapter Twelve

Not wanting to spook the man, Jerry parked down the street from the Stringers' house. He was close enough to see the house but far enough away to avoid suspicion. At least he hoped that to be the case as he currently sat leaned back in the front seat listening to Joe Bonamassa while watching the man push-mow a yard that could easily accommodate a riding mower. Since he wasn't in a hurry, and the yard indeed needed a mow, Jerry elected to stay in the Durango guiltlessly watching the man work. Jerry wasn't overly concerned about the man spotting him and making a run for it as Gunter was conducting his own stakeout under a tree in the man's yard.

His cell rang. Jerry looked at the screen. *Fred.* Jerry turned down the music and answered the call. "You know, my own mother doesn't nag me as much as you do."

"I just got another call from Stringer's wife. She said you aren't there yet. You left thirty minutes ago. What's the holdup?"

"It's supposed to rain tomorrow." Jerry waited

for the man to spool up.

"What's the weather got to do with you questioning Stringer?"

"Everything. He's cutting his grass. If he doesn't get it done today, he will be in big trouble."

"Why is he going to be in trouble?"

"The dude's grass is nearly six inches long, and he's cutting it with a push mower. It gets wet, he'll never get through it with that mower of his."

"You're kidding, right?"

"Nope."

"And you're going to just sit there and watch him mow the grass?"

"Yep."

"If you feel this strongly, maybe you should help him."

"He's doing fine on his own. Besides, working in the yard is supposed to be therapeutic. Something tells me the guy could use some Zen."

"The guy needs a bullet in his..."

Jerry cut him off. "The guy needs to finish cutting his grass. Besides, he'll be too tired to run when he sees me coming."

"I thought Marines like to run?"

"I've already had my run for the day."

"I thought you said you slept in."

"No. I said I was taking a shower. You assumed I slept in."

Where'd you run to?"

"The aquarium."

"That's a nice little jaunt."

Not compared to his usual run, but that he hadn't been running lately had worked him. "I was peeking in the front gates. What is in the enclosure to the right of the entrance?"

Fred didn't answer.

"You still there?"

"Yeah, I'm here. It is the beluga whale tank. I took Angie there the day before she went missing. It was one of her favorite exhibits."

It still is. Jerry decided to wait to tell the man that.

"Why?"

"Why what?"

"Why'd you ask about the exhibit?"

"Gunter keyed on it."

"You think maybe he knew she was there?"

Jerry decided to keep his answer short to keep questions at a minimum. "Yep."

"That's some dog you've got there, McNeal."

"I couldn't agree more."

"You're not going to let Stringer get away without questioning him, will you?"

"He's not going anywhere. You'll have your truth today." Jerry promised. He ended the call knowing full well the truth might not be the answer the man was hoping for. Jerry sighed. From what Stringer's wife had told him, Fred had crossed many lines in his bid for justice. The truth of the matter was that Jerry knew full well that if put in the same position, he himself would have done the same or maybe even worse.

Jerry concentrated on the dog. *What do you think, Gunter? Is he the one responsible for the kid's disappearance?*

Gunter turned and stared in his direction for several seconds before turning his attention back to Nick. Jerry turned up the music, biding his time.

***

Jerry waited for Nick to move to the last row before starting the engine and putting the Durango into gear. He crept forward, turning into the driveway just as the man finished. Nick didn't show any sign of bolting – a good thing, as Gunter was standing at the ready – watching as Nick slowly pushed the mower into the garage.

Nick had traded the mower for a shop towel when he reappeared and walked to Jerry like a man without a care in the world. His hair was long and pulled into a man bun. His earlobes were devoid of gauges and sat puckered against the side of his head. He waited until Jerry got out before speaking. "My lawyer told me I don't have to talk to anyone."

That explained the man's relaxed demeanor. Jerry nodded his head in agreement. "That's right."

Nick continued to wipe the sweat from his brow. "If you know that, why are you here?"

Jerry wanted nothing more than to tell the guy he'd already said more than he should and that the first thing he should've done was go inside and call his attorney. However, doing so wouldn't bode well for either of them, especially since Jerry's initial reading of the guy didn't find him involved in the child's disappearance. Still, he owed it to all involved to be sure.

Before Jerry could answer, Beverly stepped out onto the porch with two bottles of water. She crossed the distance and handed them each one. "His name's Jerry McNeal, and he's here because I called him."

Nick unscrewed the cap and took a long drink of the chilled water before answering her. "Why is he here?" Not waiting for her to answer, he repeated his question to Jerry. "Why are you here?"

"He came to hear the truth," Beverly answered for him. "You just need to tell him."

Nick blew out an exasperated sigh. "Dangit, Bev, I've already told the truth. I told it to you and everyone else who has asked. The lawyer said I don't have to tell it no more."

"This is different, Nicky. This man can make everyone leave us alone."

Nick narrowed his eyes. "What makes you so different?"

"He's a psychic. He'll know if you're telling the truth."

Nick smirked and shook his head. "Oh, Bev.

You're not buying into this nonsense, are you?"

"It's true, Nicky. Mr. Jefferies sent him. He said he would take this man's word. He said if Mr. McNeal says you are innocent, he will leave us alone."

Nick's shoulders slumped. "Bev, can't you see they are playing you? This guy is going to say I'm guilty. It's his job. Mr. Jefferies wouldn't have sent him if he didn't think he was going to get what he wanted. The man's had it out for me ever since that little girl disappeared. I told him I had nothing to do with her disappearance, yet he won't listen. He's cost me my job. My dignity. I can't even go into town without people whispering behind my back. And some don't even bother whispering. And for what? Helping out one of your friends."

As the man spoke, Jerry felt the truth in his words. *He's innocent*. Jerry firmed his chin. "What if I told you I believe you?"

"I'd say it's some kind of trick. You want me to let my guard down and say something I might regret."

Jerry unscrewed the cap from his water bottle and took a drink before answering. "Did you have anything to do with the girl's disappearance?"

Nick pointed the water bottle at him. "See, there you go, trying to trick me."

"No, I'm asking you a direct question. Did you have anything to do with Angie's disappearance?"

"No. I did not."

Jerry smiled. "I believe you."

Nick glanced at Bev and then back at Jerry. "What's the catch?"

"No catch. I believe you."

"So we're done here?"

"Not quite. I still would like to hear about your day."

"Nothing to tell. All I've been doing is cutting the grass."

"Not this day. The day the girl went missing."

"Why? You already said you believe me."

"I do. Now I need to find out why they think you were involved with her disappearance so I can convince them you're innocent."

"Can't you just tell them?"

Perhaps, if the missing child were someone other than Fred's niece, Jerry thought. Besides, he was holding on to the hope that maybe something the man said could help him figure out what actually happened to the child. "I can. I'm not sure it will be enough, though. I need to be able to convince them. But before that, I need you to walk me through that day."

"How am I supposed to do that?"

Jerry placed his hand on the man's shoulder and looked him in the eye. "Just by telling me the truth. Nothing more, nothing less. I want you to tell me everything that happened that day."

"It was over a year ago."

Jerry leveled a look at the man. "Are you going to stand there and tell me you haven't relived that day in your mind each day since?"

Nick shook his head. "No."

"Okay then, where would you like to chat?"

Nick glanced over his shoulder. "I have some chairs in the garage."

Jerry let go of Nick's shoulder. "Lead the way."

Beverly tapped Jerry on the back and waited for him to acknowledge her. "I'd like to listen in if you don't mind."

Jerry extended his hand toward the garage. "After you, ma'am." Beverly started toward the garage. Jerry followed with Gunter at his side. Beverly took the chair beside her husband, and Jerry pulled the other chair around so he was facing them.

Gunter lay on the ground by Jerry's feet. That the dog lay with his head resting on the concrete floor gave credence to the man's professed innocence. Jerry pulled out his notepad and took the lead. "Okay, so tell me everything that happened from the moment you got up until the police came to your door."

Nick stuck his finger in the hole of his earlobe and whittled it around. "I woke up and saw Bev lying there all na…"

Jerry interrupted the guy. "Let's stick to things that happened outside the bedroom unless they are pertinent to the case."

Nick shrugged. "Okay. So after we got done doing what we did in the bedroom, Bev's phone rang. It was her friend Lacey. Lacey's sewer had backed up, and she wanted to know if I'd see if I could fix it."

Jerry interrupted him. "You're a handyman. Do you always take plumbing calls?"

"Not always, but it had been raining for days, and everyone in the area was having some kind of trouble. The plumbers were busy, and because it was Bev's friend, I said I'd come take a look." He sighed. "Worst decision of my life."

Jerry looked up from his note keeping. "Why's that?"

"Because Lacey lives a few houses down from where the girl went missing."

Jerry nodded his understanding. "So you went to the house."

"I had breakfast first. Do you want to hear about that?"

Jerry ran a hand over his head. "No, let's start with you going to Lacey's house."

"Yeah, the other cops didn't want to hear it either. Anyway, I went to her house and the mess was bad. I'm telling you, I almost left without checking it out. I think Lacey knew it on account of she offered to pay me extra. So I went down in the basement, and what I saw could give a grown man nightmares."

"Nicky has a weak stomach," Beverly offered, coming to the man's defense. That she even bothered boded well for their relationship. "I shouldn't have even asked him. This is all my fault."

"It is not, and I'm tired of you taking the blame, so knock it off."

"So the toilet had backed up?" Jerry asked.

Nick looked at him. "Man, that's putting it lightly. They have three bathrooms in that house, one on each floor. Near as I could tell, they'd all been used that day, and everything ended up on the basement floor. I'm not a plumber. I don't have a special poop suit to fight that crap." Finding humor in his words, he laughed. "Anyway, I asked Lacey for some bags, you know, so that I could put them over my shoes. She brought me some of those plastic bags you get from the grocery store. I put them over my shoes and used duct tape to hold them in place. So here I am walking through this black sludge and using my snake to… not a real snake – it's this device made to unclog drains."

"Yeah, I know what a snake is," Jerry told the man.

"Anyway, I was doing that and thinking how I was going to just throw the thing away when I was finished. And everything was good, and the stuff in the toilet was going down, and so I thought I'd man up and clean the floor a little, so Lacey didn't have to. Plus, I get paid by the hour, and she'd already promised to pay extra…I guess I thought since I was already down here, why not get paid a little more, since the job was so gross and all.

"About that time, she called down the stairs and said how she had to run out for a bit and asked if I needed anything. I didn't, and that was that. So I spend the better part of the next hour scooping up crap. The thing is, the more I scooped, the slipperier things got and I fell. Right there in all that crap! And when I tried to get up, I fell again. I'm sure if anyone had been standing there, they would have laughed, but I wasn't laughing as it was nasty, and I couldn't get up. The harder I tried, the more crap I got on me." Nick shivered, and the skin near his mouth grew white in the retelling. "So I'm covered with the stuff. I go out to my truck and peel down to my skivvies. Then I look around and don't see anyone, so I peel out of those too. It's raining again by this time, but it ain't enough. So, I toss my coveralls in the back of my truck and use the back hose to rinse off. Then I grab my other pair from the truck and put them on. I didn't have any clean skivvies, so I had to go all natural under them. I normally don't have extra coveralls. But those were dirty before I left the house. I knew I'd be working in crap and thought maybe I should take an extra pair. Anyway, by then, I'd cleaned up most of the mess and figured Lacey could do the rest as I wasn't going back in there."

"So you left before she got home?"

"No, I was just getting ready to when she pulled in. She made a comment about my hair being all wet and noticed that I'd changed my clothes."

"You said you'd switched from one pair of coveralls to another. How did she know?"

"That's what I keep trying to tell everyone. Bev had made me an egg sandwich for breakfast. Only she didn't get the yellow cooked all the way. So when I bit into it, I got egg yolk all over the front. Since I was going to be working in crap, I didn't see the need to change it just yet. When I got to Lacey's house, she'd made a comment about me having egg on my face, and I said yeah, I have it on my coveralls too. We even laughed about it. Though I guess it wasn't really all that funny."

Jerry sighed. "So that is why she mentioned to the police that you'd changed your coveralls."

Nick shrugged. "I guess so."

"What did you do then?"

"I left."

"Were the police at the house down the street when you left?"

Nick nodded. "Yeah. They were there."

"Did you stop to see what was going on?"

"No. On any other day, I might have, but I was too freaked out about what had just happened. You see, when I was trying to get up, I scratched my arm, and all I kept thinking was how much trouble I'd get in if I didn't get that wound clean."

Beverly spoke up. "It's true. We watch a lot of ER reruns. You don't want to get stuff like that in an open wound, or they might have to cut your arm off."

Gunter groaned, and Jerry struggled to keep from doing the same as Nick picked up his story. "I went straight home and took a shower, but no matter how hard I scrubbed, I didn't feel clean. So I grabbed Bev's scissors and cut my hair."

"My good crafting scissors at that. Boy, was I mad." She hauled off and punched him in the shoulder.

Nick grabbed his arm. "Ow. What was that for?"

"Because I forgot all about it until now. What with the police saying you did what you did and all. Now that I know you ain't guilty, I can punch you for it."

Jerry ran his hand over his head. "What happened after you cut your hair?"

"I looked in the mirror and thought *this will never do*. I knew it would grow back, so, I went ahead and shaved it. Then I jumped back in the shower and stayed there until we ran out of hot water. Then I remembered I'd thrown my coveralls in the back of the truck, and so I drove over to Westerly to go to the car wash."

"Why Westerly? Isn't there a car wash in town?"

"Yes, but I would have had to pay for that. I have

an account with the one in Westerly – I used to do a lot of jobs over there. Anyway, I figured if I didn't feel clean after one shower that my truck wouldn't be clean after one wash. Since my account is for unlimited washes, I decide to go there. I was right. I drove through three times. I did two with my coveralls in the back of the truck and decided I didn't ever want to wear them again, so I threw them away and went through again. After I was done, I stopped and bought some of that antibacterial soap. When I got home, I took another shower. I was just getting out when the police showed up at my door and started asking all those questions. You don't want me to tell you what they asked, do you? Because there were so many questions, I don't think I can remember them all."

Jerry looked through his notes. "No. I have enough."

Nick leaned forward in his chair. "It's the truth – every word of it. Do you believe me?"

Beverly shoved both hands under her legs, and Jerry knew without seeing that her fingers were crossed as she stared straight ahead, awaiting his answer.

"I do. I knew you were innocent before you even told your story." Jerry stuffed the notebook into his pocket and pushed from the chair. "I will speak with Mr. Jefferies and make him understand. I will also see to it the town learns of your innocence so that you can get your life back."

Nick balled his hand into a fist and pressed it to his mouth as he struggled to retain control of his emotions. Beverly wasn't as successful. Her shoulders heaved as she burst into uncontrolled tears.

Chapter Thirteen

Jerry knew better than to go directly to Fred with the news. Even though thc man had promised to accept his findings, the guy would always harbor doubt. No, the only way Jerry was going to fully clear Nick of any wrongdoing would be to find Angie and have the child lead them to her abductor.

Jerry pulled his seatbelt around and looked at Gunter. "I need you to find Angie."

Gunter cocked his head to the side.

"The little girl you were playing with today." Jerry recalled what his grandmother had said. "Find Angel, Gunter. We need to find Angel."

Gunter barked and disappeared.

Jerry pushed his head into the back of the seat. *Well, crap. Maybe I should have been a little more specific.* He started the Durango and backed out of the driveway. As he did, the hairs on the back of his neck tingled. *Okay, that's more like it.* Jerry put the SUV into drive and followed the pull.

It didn't come as much of a surprise when the feeling took him the same route he'd run a few hours earlier and pulled him into the parking lot of the aquarium. Jerry parked, paid the attendant, and used his newly purchased ticket to enter the gate that had kept him out before.

The aquarium was crowded. Jerry reached inside his pocket, removed his Bluetooth, and settled the device onto his ear to give him cover should he have an opportunity to speak with the elusive spirit. He joined the crowd at the rail, standing precisely where he'd seen the child, and looked over the side just in time to see a small white beluga whale glide by. The whale swam straight toward the enclosure, curving at the last moment and heading back the way it came. A second beluga swam to the side, pushed partway out of the water, and made a noise much like a squeaky toy, to the delight of those watching.

Jerry took out his phone and snapped a photo so he could send it to Max later. Seeing no sign of Angie or Gunter, he used the pull and found them standing at the touch tank watching as a little boy dipped his hand into the water and picked up a starfish. Jerry stepped up next to her and kept his voice low. "Hello, Angie."

Angie ignored him.

"I'm sorry. I forgot. Your name is Angel now, isn't it?"

She turned to him with wide eyes and nodded her head.

"I'm a friend. Can we go somewhere where we can talk?"

The boy standing next to her lowered the starfish and pointed directly at him. “Stranger danger! Stranger danger!”

An employee in a navy blue polo standing on the other side of the tank narrowed her eyes at him.

Crap. Jerry held up his hands. “I was just standing here.”

The woman continued what she was doing while watching him from the corner of her eye.

Angie turned and ran to a nearby fish tank with Gunter following close behind. Jerry followed.

“Come on, kiddo. I really need you to take a walk with me.”

The little boy who’d been standing next to him earlier peeked around the side, saw Jerry, and pointed once more. “Stranger danger! Stranger danger!”

Jerry looked to see the same woman in the blue polo talk into a handheld radio. *Crap*. Jerry pulled out his cell, swiped to find Fred’s number and typed his message. > “Come to aquarium.” Realizing Fred would probably bombard him with a multitude of questions regarding his chat with Nick, he added > “Bring bail money.” And hit send.

Tiring of the fish tank, Angie moved to another exhibit. The problem was she seemed to be following the same boy who appeared to be there with a group of students. Though the chaperones now gazed at Jerry with wary glances, no one had actually called him out on the fact he appeared to be targeting the boy.

Jerry knelt next to Angie, who was annoyingly hovering next to the boy. "Uncle Fred wants to talk to you. He sent me to find you. We have to go now."

Angie's face lit up.

The boy beside her didn't seem as delighted with the news as his face turned beet red. "I DON'T HAVE AN UNCLE FRED! I'M NOT GOING WITH YOU!"

Gunter joined in with ghostly barks as Angie blinked her confusion.

Way to go, Marine. You can now add suspected pedophile to your portfolio. Ready to abort the current mission, Jerry stood. As he turned, he came face to face with two aquarium security guards.

The taller of the guards grabbed him by the arm, and Gunter's barks turned to snarls.

"Easy, fella, it's okay."

The guard firmed his grip. "I'm not your fella, and what you're trying to do here is not okay."

While Jerry wanted to struggle out of the man's grip, he knew any movement that showed him to be in distress would set off the dog. "Ease your hold, man. I'm not resisting you."

The guard kept his grip until they led Jerry outside, then let him go as both men faced him. The only good thing that came of them taking him outside was Angie had followed. *Of course she followed. She's Fred's niece. She's probably hoping to see you get tasered.*

"Let's see some ID, pal," the one who'd led him out ordered.

"It's in my hip pocket." As he reached for his wallet, Jerry was glad he'd elected to leave his pistol under his driver's seat. He took his driver's license from his wallet and handed it to the guy. "I'm a Pennsylvania State Police Officer."

"I don't care who you are. That don't give you any right to mess with kids." Guard one snatched the ID from him and read Jerry's credentials into the radio before handing it back.

Jerry returned the ID to his wallet and decided to go on the defensive and hopefully stall long enough for Fred to arrive. "What do you mean messing with kids? I didn't touch anyone."

"No. But you were talking to him. Trying to get him to go with you."

"Is that what this is all about." Jerry smiled and tilted his head to show the Bluetooth. "The kid was mistaken. I was on the phone."

The head guard looked at the other guy and then back to Jerry. "If you're a cop, let's see your badge?"

Jerry shoved his hands into his pants pockets and smiled a sheepish grin. "I lost it."

"What do you mean you lost it?"

"Just what I said. Give it a minute, and you'll hear for yourself."

Sure enough, the voice on the other end backed up his story.

The main guard laughed. "Boy, I bet that caused some ribbing from the boys. Probably got you a suspension as well."

A permanent one. Jerry nodded. "You have no idea."

"Listen, I don't mean to give you a hard time, but we can't have you freaking out the kids like that."

Jerry looked at Angie. "Yeah, I'm supposed to meet my friend Fred in the parking lot. Maybe I'll just go and come back later."

Angie disappeared. Gunter looked at Jerry, whined, and then he too was gone.

"Okay. Maybe you should bring your own kid next time. That way, you won't seem so creepy."

Jerry sighed as the guards followed him to the front gate. He was relieved to see Fred's town car pulling into the lot as he cleared the gates. If the guards were still watching, it backed up his story. Jerry looked for Angie and Gunter. Neither were in sight.

Fred pulled to the curb and rolled down the window. "This better be good."

Jerry heard giggling and looked inside the car to see Angie and Gunter sitting in the back seat. Not wishing to lose sight of the childish spirit, he opened the passenger side door and got inside. "Let's go somewhere we can talk."

Fred's jaw twitched, but he pulled away from the curb without speaking. He took a right out of the parking lot and made a left on Greenmanville Avenue. Jerry figured they were going back to the house.

Just past the cemetery, Fred slowed and parked at the far end of the small ice cream parking lot Jerry had noticed earlier in the day.

Fred shrugged. "I like ice cream. It calms my nerves."

Angie clapped her hands. Gunter barked his agreement. Jerry suddenly found himself wondering if the place served anything stronger.

Fred ordered a strawberry sundae. Jerry opted for a banana split, and they walked to a picnic table that overlooked the river.

Fred looked at him over his spoon. "Now that we're alone, what was the business at the aquarium?"

The truth of the matter was they were more alone in the vehicle. Not only were the neighboring tables occupied, but Angie now sat next to Fred with two swirl cones in her hand. One she was eating, and the other she held down for Gunter, who was carefully licking and seemed to be very much enjoying the frosty delight.

Jerry turned his attention to Fred. "First things first."

Fred waved him off. "If you're talking about

Nick, I already know he's innocent."

Jerry leveled a look at the man. "If you know he's innocent, why are you bent on ruining the man's life?"

"Cool your jets, McNeal. I didn't know until today."

Jerry rolled his neck from side to side. "I'm not following you."

"It's easy. If you thought Stringer was guilty, you would have called a long time ago."

"Are you willing to accept my word on it?"

"I told you I would."

"That's not what I asked."

"I'll back off."

Jerry lowered his voice. "Not just back off. I want you all the way off. You're not even to go near the man other than to apologize for what you've put him and his family through."

Fred nodded and went back to his ice cream. Jerry tapped his fingers on the table.

Fred paused. His mouth twitched. "I take it you've found her."

Jerry smiled and nodded toward where the child sat.

Fred's brows knit. He bit at his bottom lip then blew out a long breath. "So Angie is in fact…"

Jerry cut him off. "She's an Angel."

Fred closed his eyes briefly, and Jerry could see the man struggling to control his emotions. He opened his eyes. "How?"

Jerry's first instinct was to tell him what happened at the aquarium but decided it was irrelevant. "I don't know yet. Your niece won't talk to me."

"Why not? I thought you were good at talking to ghosts."

Angie's spirit pulsed in and out. "I'm not a ghost. I'm an angel!"

"I know, honey. Uncle Fred didn't mean anything by it."

Fred looked from the bench to Jerry. "What did I do wrong? What didn't I mean?"

"Angie."

Angie drew her lips together. "I'm not Angie. I'm an angel."

Gunter woofed and tilted his head as if to say, *You're not very good at dealing with children, are you?*

Jerry pushed his dish aside and ran both hands through his hair. Calmer, he began again. "She doesn't want to be called Angie. She wants to be called Angel."

"Because that's what I am." Angie beamed her delight.

Jerry smiled back and repeated her words. "Because that's what she is."

Fred pushed his cup to the side. "You said she wouldn't talk to you. Why is she talking to you now?"

No clue. "I don't know."

"Can't you ask her?"

"You just did."

"You mean she can hear me?"

"Of course I can. The boy said he was stranger danger."

Jerry smiled. "She wasn't supposed to talk to strangers."

Fred chuckled. "I taught her that. Now what's she saying?"

"Nothing."

"What do you mean nothing? Why ain't she answering?" Fred turned to the spot Jerry indicated. "Why aren't you answering Uncle Fred?"

"Why'd you make Mommy stay home?"

"She wants to know why you made her mom stay home."

"She knows Sarah is in town?"

Angie nodded. "Yes. She wanted to come, and Uncle Fred told her no."

The little girl's energy was changing, and Jerry was afraid her spirit would leave. "Fred. Angel said her mother wanted to come, but you made her stay at the house. She doesn't sound happy. Maybe we should all go back to the house so we can find out what happened?"

"I don't know. I haven't said anything to Sarah about this."

"Mommy knows."

"She said her mother knows."

Fred hesitated for several moments before finally shaking his head and hefting his legs over the bench seat. As he stood, he handed Jerry the keys. "You mind driving?"

"Not at all." As they walked to the car, Jerry looked to see what was keeping Gunter.

The dog now stood in the middle of the table lapping ice cream from Jerry's plastic bowl. Jerry keyed the door unlocked and walked back to the table to retrieve the bowls they'd left. He smiled at Gunter. "So you do eat."

Gunter licked his lips and wagged his tail.

***

Jerry stood in the back yard waiting to be invited inside. Gunter sat next to him, and Jerry hoped Angie's spirit was inside. If not, he would have nothing more to offer as Fred was inside telling what they knew thus far. The back door opened. Fred waved them inside.

"She took it better than I thought. She said Angie came to her in a dream and told her. That's why she came here today to tell me. Can you believe that?"

Jerry clasped Fred on the shoulder and nodded. "It doesn't surprise me at all."

Fred led the way into the room. "Jerry McNeal, this is my sister."

Dressed in slacks and a short-sleeved sweater,

Sarah's thin face looked drawn and pale. She reached a hand to Jerry without rising from the couch. Jerry wondered if she was too emotionally drained to make an effort or if some internal motherly instinct told her that her daughter was sitting next to her.

"Nice to meet you, ma'am." Jerry let go of her hand and took a seat on the opposite side of the room.

Angie patted the spot beside her. Gunter jumped onto the couch, tucked in his paws, and lay next to the girl with his head in her lap.

"Freddy has told me a lot about you, Mr. McNeal."

Jerry looked at Fred and smiled. "I'm sure Freddy has had a lot to say."

"He tells me you travel with a ghost dog."

Jerry leaned back in his chair and intertwined his fingers. "He said that, did he?"

"He did."

"And you believed him?"

She smiled, and her face transformed. "Of course. Freddy has never lied to me. He's a man of his word. If he tells you something, you can be sure he's telling the truth."

Jerry tapped his thumbs together. "Good to know."

"He told me you can see spirits."

"I can."

"I believe you. While I can't see them, I sometimes know they are near, like now. I can feel Angie. She's sitting next to me, isn't that right?"

"She is." Jerry saw the woman's shoulders relax and wondered if she'd really felt the child's spirit or merely wanted very much for it to be so.

"I'm not Angie."

It's show time. Jerry took a deep breath. "She's ready. I never know how much time we have with them, so we should begin. You can ask questions. I must ask you to choose your words carefully so we can keep contact with her. If I put up my hand, it means she is unhappy with the question. Rephrase it and ask again. She can hear us, so I won't be repeating the questions. I will tell you her answers as she tells them. First, I will tell you she does not wish to be called Angie anymore."

Sarah's brow creased. "Why not? Don't you like the name?"

"I used to be Angie, but I'm an angel."

Jerry repeated her words.

Sarah took a deep breath and blew it out again. "Are you sad?"

"Not anymore. Not since Nona found me."

Jerry repeated Angie's words and looked at Sarah. "Who's Nona?"

Sarah's eyes widened, and she narrowed her eyes at Fred. "You told him to say that."

Fred threw his hands up. "I did no such thing."

"They're fighting again. Mommy was mad at Uncle Fred the day I went away. She called him some bad words." Angie placed her hands to her ears.

Jerry held up his hands. "She's not happy you two are arguing. She said it was like this the day she went away. She said her mom called Uncle Fred some bad words and she had to cover her ears."

Sarah blinked back tears. "Earmuffs."

"What?"

"That is what we said when we wanted to say something she wasn't supposed to hear. It doesn't prove anything. Everyone with kids has heard that term."

Jerry thought to remind her he didn't have any kids. "I haven't."

Angie frowned. "Only Mom was mad at Uncle Fred and forgot to say it."

"She said you were too mad at Fred to remind her to cover her ears."

"I don't believe it." Though she said the words, Jerry could tell she wanted to believe.

Angie placed her hand on Sarah's leg. "Uncle Fred didn't tell you to come today. Nona did. After I visited you in your dream. She said if you come, you'd know I was okay."

Jerry repeated Angie's words, and Sarah's face paled.

Angie continued. "Don't be sad, Mommy. I'm

not mad about the baby either. I'm an angel now. I can help you and Daddy watch over him."

Fred blinked his surprise. "You're pregnant?"

Sarah nodded.

Anyone else would feel this moment to be magical. To Jerry, it suddenly felt as if he was watching an episode of Dr. Phill. He ran a hand over his head, then sat back in his chair, intertwined his fingers, and tapped his thumbs together. His therapist would have a field day with this. Jerry laughed to himself. *It's a good thing I stopped seeing the man, or he'd have me fitted for a straitjacket.*

Chapter Fourteen

Angie nodded her willingness as Gunter moved to Jerry's side. Jerry looked at both Fred and Sarah. "I think it is time to find out what happened to her if you're ready."

Fred looked to Sarah, who took a deep breath and closed her eyes. She opened them once more. "I'm ready."

Jerry wasted no time with preliminaries. "Angel, what happened to you?"

"You mean the day I went away?"

"Yes."

"It stopped raining, and I wanted to go out and play." As she relayed her story, Jerry repeated her words. "I wanted to find the kitty."

Sarah frowned. "What kitty?"

"The one Uncle Fred and I saw cross the road."

Jerry looked at Fred. "She was chasing after the cat you and she saw cross the road."

"The cat?"

"Yes, the one that lives in the woods."

"She said it lives in the woods." Jerry offered.

Fred wrinkled his brow, then lifted his head.

"The Fisher cat. It's not a real cat, more like a weasel. They're native to the area."

"I went through the woods 'cause that's where we saw him go. It started to rain, and I couldn't remember how to find Uncle Fred. I heard a noise. I saw it was the cat, so I followed him. He went in a hole. It was big, and I thought maybe he had babies, so I crawled in to see. I wasn't scared. Not at first. Then the mud covered me, and everything went dark. When I woke up, I was an angel." By the time she finished the telling, she was covered in mud. As often happened, the image only lasted long enough for Jerry to see the truth in her story.

Jerry struggled to repeat her words. When he'd finished, he realized he was crying. He wiped the moisture from his eyes with his hands as he recalled what Nick had said about the rain. More tears flowed as he realized the man's life had been turned upside down simply because he'd been willing to do a good deed for a friend.

Jerry looked at Fred, his voice breaking as he spoke. "It wasn't anyone's fault. It sounds as if she found either a large animal den or small cave. When she went inside to investigate, it collapsed, trapping her inside. It doesn't sound as if she suffered."

Sarah clutched her hands to her shoulders and wept silently as his words sank in.

Fred covered his face with his hands. His sobs were more profound.

Gunter lifted his head and joined their mourning with a soulful howl.

From her place on the couch, Angie cupped her mouth with her hands, giggling as she mimicked the tune.

***

It didn't take long to find the body, now that they knew where to look. Of course, having Gunter to lead in the search didn't hurt. Jerry wanted nothing more than to leave, as he didn't like this part of the job. But he felt he owed it to Fred to stay and lend emotional support. Angie stood next to her mother. One hand clutched the woman's skirt, with a finger of the other hand tucked into her mouth as they both watched the team carefully remove the dirt.

Gunter leaned into Jerry's leg, a welcomed show of support.

"We've got her," someone yelled.

Sarah turned to Fred, and they both held each other and cried.

Jerry felt a tug on his pants and looked to see Angie standing there. He looked around and then knelt to hear what the child had to say.

"Why are they crying?"

"They are sad you went away."

"But I'm right here."

Jerry sighed. "I'm afraid the going away part is harder for the people left behind."

"I wish they could still see me." She scratched

Gunter on the head. "How come you're the only one who can see us?"

Jerry started to tell her he wasn't the only one but knew it would only serve to further confuse her. He smiled. "I guess I'm just lucky that way."

***

Lost in his thoughts, Jerry walked to the aquarium to pick up his ride. He could have easily asked Fred for a ride, but the energy in the house was that of a somewhat comforted knowledge, and Jerry didn't want to risk disturbing the mood. After he picked up the Durango, he drove to the next lot and parked at Olde Mystic Village. Though he'd passed the quaint little village multiple times, he'd yet to take the time to explore any of the shops. He got out, hoping to unwind by picking up a few souvenirs. Gunter ran ahead, nose to the ground. It didn't escape Jerry that the K-9 seemed to be lighter in his step. It led him to wonder if this task had weighed as heavily on his ghostly companion as it had him.

You're reaching for things, McNeal. Maybe so, but the energy around the dog did seem lighter. They turned the corner, and Gunter froze in place. A second later, he hopped a small rail fence, sniffing a large green gnome statue. Satisfied the figure didn't mean any harm, the dog raced off to see what else there was to see.

Jerry left the dog to his own devices, ducked into a Christmas shop, bought a couple of ornaments that caught his eye, then went into a mystical shop and picked up a few crystals for Savannah. By the time he left the village, he'd added a couple of frogs for his mom to add to her collection, puzzles for Max, and a painted teapot and cup without any clue who he'd purchased them for. The six-inch chunk of chocolate peanut butter fudge was his and his alone.

As Jerry returned to his ride, Gunter appeared next to him, jumping into the passenger seat the moment Jerry opened the door. The dog's tongue hung from his mouth, leaving Jerry to wonder what the K-9 had been up to. As he crossed the parking lot, Jerry noticed a red Mini Cooper parked near one of the buildings.

Jerry cocked an eye toward his partner. Gunter's lip curled up ever so slightly, showing the unmistakable K-9 smile.

Jerry shook his head and momentarily envied his companion's escapades.

Gunter barked as they neared the ice cream shop. Jerry chuckled as he wheeled the Durango into the parking spot. Either the dog had worked up an appetite or had just discovered a new fondness for the creamy delight. Either way, Jerry decided a little ice cream couldn't hurt.

He ordered himself another banana split and a cup of vanilla for Gunter, thinking they'd eat in the Durango. As he turned to leave, he saw Ralf and Emily sitting at the same table he and Fred had occupied earlier in the day.

Ralf raised his hand, motioning him over. As Jerry approached, he noticed the couple was not eating ice cream. Instead, their plates were heaped with breakfast food. Jerry looked at his banana boat and frowned. As much as he enjoyed ice cream, the scrambled eggs and bacon that took up much of Ralf's plate made his stomach rumble.

Jerry slid onto the bench opposite the couple. "I didn't know this place served breakfast."

Ralf lifted a crispy stick and pointed it at him as he spoke. "They don't. Not anymore. This place used to have the best breakfast in town. We still come here every now and then, and being on the other side, can have whatever we want."

Emily smiled the smile of a much younger woman. "I was craving scrambled eggs with herbs, and Ralf agreed to bring me here when he came back."

Ralf shoved another slice of bacon into his mouth. "Yep, only gone half a day and decided I missed the old gal. I think she missed me too, as she's agreed to travel some with me while the grandkids are in school."

Emily nodded. "It's true. I did. Ralf and I are going to the Smoky Mountains to scare the bears."

Jerry was in the process of taking a bite of banana and hesitated. "Do you mean see the bears?"

"Anyone can see them. What's the fun in that?

We're just going to give them a little scare." Emily winked. "I don't see any harm in that, do you, Mr. McNeal?"

Jerry hesitated once more as he tried to recall if he'd told the couple his name.

Emily reached over the table and patted his hand. "Your reputation precedes you, Mr. McNeal. Why, when spirits find out what you did to help me and Ralf, they will all be wanting a session with you."

Jerry's mouth went dry. "I'm not a marriage counselor or any other counselor, for that matter."

Emily's eyes twinkled. "You don't give yourself enough credit, Mr. McNeal. I can't remember a time when me and Ralf have been this happy."

Appetite lost, Jerry pushed his banana boat to the side and watched as Gunter jumped onto the table to finish it. Jerry pulled the dish away and sat it on the ground. Gunter jumped down, chasing the dish with his tongue. As soon as he finished, Jerry waved goodbye to Ralf and Emily, and retrieved the containers, tossing both into the trash as he returned to his SUV.

Once inside, Jerry turned toward Gunter. "I'm not a marriage counselor. Get it? I don't know how this other side business works, but I want you to spread the word."

Gunter barked and promptly disappeared.

Jerry passed Pearl Street and parked in an open spot in front of Mystic Pizza. Though he'd initially only intended to get a photo of the sign, the smell of the pizza wafting through the air lured him inside. He was seated upstairs near a window overlooking the town and was immediately caught up in the atmosphere of the place. The bottom half of the walls were shiplap, the top adorned with movie star photos. Some were headshots. Others showed well-known actors in various movie scenes. He snapped a few pictures, setting his phone aside when the waitress approached with a menu.

He waved off the menu. “Large pepperoni and a Bud.”

She tucked the menu under her arm and smiled. “You got it.”

“Hey?” he called as she started to walk away. “Is that *Mystic Pizza* playing on the television?”

Her mouth twitched. Jerry could tell she was trying not to laugh as she pointed to the wording on her black t-shirt. “You’ve come to the right place. If we’re open, that’s what's on.”

Jerry waited for her to walk away and snapped a few photos of Julia Roberts from the television. He sent them to Max.

She responded immediately. > “Cool! You’re watching the movie.”

He chuckled. > “Not exactly. I’m sitting in Mystic Pizza waiting for my pizza.”

Max. > “Lucky! I just told Mom. She is major jealous. She said you get to do all the cool stuff!”

Jerry looked at the empty chair across from him. *Depends on your definition of cool.*

The couple at the table next to him sat close and spoke too low for him to hear. On the street below, he could see families walking and talking excitedly with their hands. Even the actor on the television screen was currently engaged in an onscreen kiss. Jerry drummed his fingers on the table, debating his response. Picking up his phone, he typed. >"Tell your mom hi and ask her what size t-shirt she wears. I'll send her one that says Mystic Pizza."

Max > "Mom said you don't need to waste your money on her… Don't tell her I told you, but she wears a medium."

Jerry looked up to see the waitress coming with his beer. > "Okay, Max. I'll talk to you soon. Take care."

Max. > "See ya. Oh, and give Gunter a hug for me."

Jerry set the phone aside and lifted his glass.

***

"McNeal?"

Jerry turned to see Fred heading his way.

Fred eyed the seabag. "You weren't planning to leave without saying goodbye, were you?"

Yes. Jerry handed him the envelope he'd planned on stuffing inside the screen door. "I was going to give you this first."

"Liar."

"Maybe."

Fred handed him a small box.

"What's this?"

"Open it and see."

Jerry pulled back the lip of the box and saw a row of white business cards. He pulled one out and read, **Jerry McNeal. Department of Defense. Lead Paranormal Investigator.** The card had Jerry's cell number on it. Jerry raised a brow. "Does the Department of Defense even have a paranormal unit?"

Fred rocked back on his heels. "They do now."

"What if I say no?"

"You won't."

"You sound pretty sure of yourself."

"No, I'm pretty sure of you. This, whatever you want to call it, is in your blood. The answers might sting a little, but they are answers people may never get if not for you and that dog of yours. Is he here? I wanted to thank him for his part in this."

Jerry pointed to where Gunter was currently standing. "He knows you're grateful."

"How can you tell?"

"Easy. He's wagging his tail."

Fred reached into his breast pocket and pulled out a smaller envelope. "You'll need this."

Jerry opened it and eyed the gold badge and credit card engraved with his name. A part of him wanted to drop it like a hot potato, but another part

– the part that was tired of being laughed at for supposedly losing a badge he'd held in high esteem – took the offering.

Fred's smile widened. "You'll use the card for all expenses. And don't stay in any dumps. You don't have to stay in the penthouse, but we don't expect to see you in any no-tell motel either. We want you to be comfortable, so the rooms you've been using are fine."

Jerry held up the badge. "This changes nothing. I'm still following the Hash Mark Killer case."

Fred smiled. "That's good, because it's your first assignment."

"What is?"

"The Hash Mark Killer case. Only now, you'll be privy to all we know."

About the Author

Sherry A. Burton writes in multiple genres and has won numerous awards for her books. Sherry's awards include the coveted Charles Loring Brace Award, for historical accuracy within her historical fiction series, The Orphan Train Saga. Sherry is a member of the National Orphan Train Society, presents lectures on the history of the orphan trains, and is listed on the NOTC Speaker's Bureau as an approved speaker.

Originally from Kentucky, Sherry and her Retired Navy Husband now call Michigan home. Sherry enjoys traveling and spending time with her husband of more than forty years.